SEA LEGS

ELEMENTS OF DANGER, BOOK 1

WILLA BROOKS

Get new release updates and exclusive content when
you sign up for my mailing list.

For my husband and son. My favorite people.

CHAPTER 1

SARAH

*P*eeking down at the display on my phone, the time read 5:37 p.m. Through the huge glass window, headlights of the passing vehicles illuminated the thick, falling snowflakes. They'd changed from light to heavy since I'd been sitting here for fifteen minutes, waiting for him.

I made a note of what I was planning to order from the menu board. My stomach rumbled. That salad I had for lunch wasn't such a great idea. I should have eaten something heartier. Luckily, no one could hear it over the patron chatter and a barista shouting customer names when their orders were ready.

Carol Lynne made me promise to try going on three dates through online dating before I abandoned the idea altogether. The first date was boring because he lied on his profile, and we had nothing in common. The second date, we nicknamed "tarantula Dave" because he was weirdly attached to his pets. Let's just say I faked a migraine and got the heck out of the café.

After a brief text with number three, we agreed to meet here. This one will be the last date I'll be required to go on to fulfill my promise. Thank goodness, because these things were a waste of time as far as I was concerned. Carol Lynne and the rest of my family needed to accept that I didn't want a relationship. I did this to please them. My heart fell as my mind headed down the road that I didn't want it to go down.

I pursed my lips at the night sky and checked my messages to make sure he didn't cancel. I shivered at the blast of cold air on my back as someone opened the door behind me. Maybe I should put on my coat again.

"You, Sarah Stevenson?"

A handsome hoodlum stood before me. He had a crew cut, dirty blond hair, azure eyes, and a sculpted face. He wore a puffy, black winter jacket with a black hoodie that was pulled up.

Something ignited in my heart, like a lit torch, and radiated warmth. That hadn't happened since Jason.

Remembering my manners, I shot out of my seat

and extended my hand for a shake. "Yes, that's me. You must be Carter Evans."

His eyes traveled my body from head to toe; his brows wrinkled like he couldn't make sense of me. His handshake was brief. He let go and took a seat.

And just like that, he extinguished the flame.

I remained standing. "Are you going to order anything?" I gestured to the order counter.

"Nah, I'm good."

My brows wrinkled. Was this man planning on watching me eat like a creeper?

"I'm going to order." I flashed him a half-hearted smile, that he didn't deserve out of ingrained politeness.

Someone rushed in front of me as I walked to the counter. I hugged myself, rubbing the sleeve of my black sweater. My knee-length black and white check-ered skirt, black stockings, and Mary Jane shoes had not been the wisest choice of clothing to wear in this weather. But I was taking a cab home anyway, so it wasn't nuts. I tucked my long brown hair behind my ear because I felt twitchy.

When it was my turn, I ordered and tapped my phone on the scanner to pay. Wait a minute. Did he have money to pay for food? Was that why he wasn't eating? Then why make a date in the first place?

Moving over to the counter's pickup side, I opened the bag, unwrapped my sandwich, and took a bite. If I finished eating before going back to the table, it wouldn't be so weird.

I was about halfway through the sandwich when the barista called my name. I grabbed it and thanked her while taking a sleeve from the counter to slip around the warm cup.

Carter's seat was empty. I glanced around the café. Did he get up to use the bathroom? I scanned the café. No sign of him. For some reason, my attention was pulled to the street. I barely caught sight of the back of his jacket as he hurried up the block. He stopped by a parked van, opened the driver's side door, turned, and looked right at me. Then he got into his van.

My throat hurt, and everything in me felt heavy.

I trudged over to the table, flopped down, and finished my dinner, trying to swallow past the lump in my throat.

On the bright side, I didn't have to miss any more shows because of these stupid dates. At least I would be safe in my apartment and not out risking my life for a bunch of losers.

Later that night, after eventually making it back to my apartment, all of my favorite shows were over. I got washed up and settled in bed. I texted Carol Lynne.

Sarah Stevenson: Strike three.

Carol Lynne Miller: Oh no. What happened?

Sarah Stevenson: He walked out on me.

Carol Lynne Miller: What?! Why? Did you guys get into a fight?

Sarah Stevenson: No. I guess he didn't like what he saw.

Carol Lynne Miller: What?! You're so pretty, no one would think that! Is he on crack?

Sarah Stevenson: Haha. Ok, we can go with that. Carter the crack up.

Carol Lynne Miller: I'll kill Keith.

Sarah Stevenson: Who's Keith?

Carol Lynne Miller: The hottie guitarist that I've been talking about.

Sarah Stevenson: Wait. What does Keith have to do with any of this?

Carol Lynne Miller: He's Keith's friend. I sometimes see them going into Keith's apartment.

Sarah Stevenson: So you just went up to him and was like, 'hey, you wanna date my friend?'

Carol Lynne Miller: Not exactly. I texted Keith and asked if he knew anyone that would be interested in going out on a date with you. Then I sent him a pic.

My brain spun at this new revelation. It took a second before I could respond.

Sarah Stevenson: Which pic?
Carol Lynne Miller: Us at the New Year's Eve party last month.

Exiting the chat, I opened the photo gallery app, and scrolled and located the picture she was referring to. I wore my black sequinned tank dress and my long brown hair was up in a bun. We were facing each other. I had one leg hiked around Carol Lynne's waist while she kept it there. One of my arms was slung around her shoulders while the other hand held onto a glass of champagne. We were at a New Year's Eve party at her PR friends' apartments, and if my hazy memory serves, we were dancing the tango.

Sarah Stevenson: No wonder he didn't like what he saw. He probably thought we catfished him.
Carol Lynne Miller: That's bullshit, Sarah. Anyone meeting you for the first time could never be disappointed. Whatever was going through his mind had nothing to do with you.
Sarah Stevenson: I'm gonna head off to bed. I'll see you tomorrow.

Carol Lynne Miller: Ok. I'll buy you lunch.

Grabbing the remote from the windowsill next to my bed, I switched on the TV that sat on a chest of drawers. I shoved the weight of the disappointment that snuck into my heart. It was my fault for hoping for a brief second that things might change.

I surfed past the evening news, stopping at a *Friends* episode where Joey's head was stuck inside a turkey and let it lull me to sleep.

CHAPTER 2

We sat across from each other at the dining tables in the café on the ground level of our office building.

"The worst part was when he turned to look back at me and got in his van." I chewed on the cob salad Carol Lynne had treated me to for lunch. I'd bought us more than a few cookies, because I needed them.

Her features were bird-like, and she had a sympathetic expression. She wore a white blazer over her black satin blouse. Her shoulder-length blond hair was combed in a clean, low ponytail. "I'm sorry. That'll teach me to ask favors from guitarists."

That stung my pride. *Please find a date for my loser friend*. She hadn't said that, but that was probably how he took it. Maybe that's why Carter wasn't interested. Perhaps he thought I might have been desperate. *Sigh.*

"Well, we tried. No more dates."

"Not even one?" Her tone was cajoling.

"No! That wasn't the agreement—one month. I've lived up to my end. Live up to yours and leave me alone about my life choices. It wasn't like I bugged you about yours. You haven't had a date in eons."

People who were sitting at the other tables stopped what they were doing and looked over at me.

My cheeks heated.

"Okay, okay. Don't bite my head off." She threw up both her hands in a surrender gesture.

Her reaction made me feel a little lighter, but I shouldn't have snapped. I bit my lip and lowered my voice, "Sorry."

She gave me a small smile that let me know that I was forgiven.

"So who's Keith? Not that I'm interested in dating him," I clarified and squinted at her.

Her lips quirked to one side. "He's in a band called McRiff that plays around the city on the weekends, and he's my neighbor. I usually see him in passing."

There was something in her tone. It was like she wanted to gush but held it back.

"You like him, don't you?"

The blush that appeared on her face told me what I wanted to know.

"So, why don't you ask him out?" I pushed.

She shrugged. "The parade of women going to and fro. How do I know he doesn't have some kind of disease?"

"Well, you have a point there, I guess. Better be sure of the guy first. I'll never understand how some women can just jump into bed with a guy who they just met."

Her lips quirked in a wry expression. "Bless your romantic heart."

Time went by quickly as we dissected the motivations for relationships between men and women. By the time I realized it, our lunchtime was over.

I brought the brown paper bag full of cookies and a cup of coffee to my desk.

While I was on the phone taking a message from a client who'd canceled their meeting, Brandy Fleming marched up to me like she was on a mission. The glee radiating from her while she performed evil acts was more akin to the wicked witch.

She stopped in front of my desk and leaned on one leg, like a runway model. Her emerald green skirt suit was a bold choice since it amplified her dyed red hair. If the Wizard of Oz ever had a rude daughter, it would be her.

I rolled my eyes, pursed my lips and entered the meeting status into the inter-office messaging system.

"Stacy. Get me coffee." Brandy's voice was shrill.

I continued typing. It was crap like this that reminded me of my alternate future where I would have been running our restaurant. But that dream had died with Jason.

"Well?" Brandy pressed.

After hanging up the phone, I picked up the name-plate on my desk, mouthed my name, then set it back down and sent a message about the meeting to the marketing department. Maybe then she'd stop mispronouncing my name.

"Get. Me. Coffee." She pivoted and strutted away.

"What are you gonna do about that?" Gerald Bertrand said from his end of the cubicle.

"Report it to HR? I've no clue how to handle this. She can't stand by my desk and scream at me all the time. Plus, it's not my job to bring her coffee. She's not even from this dang department. What the heck does she have against me?"

His grunt was his only response as his fingers went back to typing.

After I filled out a complaint form in HR on the second floor, I went to the café on the ground floor to buy another bag of cookies. As I turned to leave, I saw Carter, standing with a woman with long black hair and a puffy black jacket that did not conceal her rounded figure. He wore the same jacket as he had on our almost-date. His attention was straight ahead, and his brows were furrowed while she gabbed. She didn't notice or didn't care that he wasn't interested in what she was saying.

She caught my stare first and glared back. The hairs on the back of my neck stood straight. Carter followed the line of her stare until our eyes met. His wince was slight before he wiped his expression clean and returned to face the front. I tore my eyes away from them and walked through the exit.

After putting my stuff on my desk, I stopped by the employee cafeteria and made Brandy's coffee. I conveniently forgot to add the sugar. After placing it on her desk and receiving a stink eye, nothing was more satisfying than the sound of her spewing it out as I walked back to my desk.

Later that evening, I climbed the flight of stairs that led to Carol Lynne's apartment. Two men were standing by the apartment at the far end of the hall. A tall, skinny one with dark hair opened the door while another guy who had his back to me waited.

I knocked on Carol Lynne's door, and they both turned at the noise. Carter glanced over his shoulder at me. My stomach fell. Sweet Jesus, I was having one of those days where I couldn't catch a break.

It didn't take long for her to open the door. *Thank God*.

Her face fell when she saw mine, and she opened the door wider to let me pass.

I hung up my coat and bag in her closet, and slipped out of my boots while she stepped out and said a polite hello to Keith.

Carter would dish or have dished to his buddy about what happened at the café.

I went to sit on Carol Lynne's couch, in what one might describe as her bohemian living room, and waited while she wrapped up her pleasantries.

After she closed the door, she went straight to her stove to spoon our vegetarian chili into bowls. Her kitchen consisted of cupboards with one countertop that flanked the fridge, a sink on one side, and a stove. All of it was against the back wall.

"There's a rumor that Brandy Fleming from finance spat out her coffee because the secretary forgot the sugar."

What?

"How did you hear?"

She switched the channel on TV from the evening news to *Wheel*. She knew me well enough to know that I hated the news because of the reports on violence.

"Maureen told me. She saw when you put the cup on her desk," my friend told me while she grabbed two bowls from the counter and brought them to the coffee table. She pulled the table a bit closer.

I got up and grabbed a stack of meditation pillows from the corner of the room. Carol Lynne came back with two glasses of wine and placed them next to our bowls, then took the pillows and set them down on the floor.

We got comfortable and dug into our chili—the smell of patchouli incense interfered with my dinner enjoyment. She'd probably burned some right before I came over.

"Why does Brandy have to demand things from me? Why couldn't she ask someone in her own department? Leaving your desk just to demand coffee is a waste of time. Ever since she got that promotion, she's been a diva."

She shrugged. "Corporate asshole bullies for you. Power corrupts. They're all the same to me. My pie offer still stands if you want to take me up on it."

On days like today, when I had to file an HR complaint because someone was yelling at me about coffee, the pie offer, which was code for setting up a pie-baking business, was more attractive.

I sighed and asked, "So, how was your day? Is Jackie still trying to steal your work?"

She rolled her eyes while taking a sip of wine. "Up to the same nonsense. If I knew that I'd resort to hiding my files on my personal cloud so that someone from work doesn't steal my ideas, I don't know if I would have gotten into this job."

"Maybe this is the nudge *you* need in the pie direction, or at least pie equivalent."

She chuckled. "Don't know if my baking prowess is good enough to match yours or my mother's, for that matter, so I'll stick to PR."

The lights and TV went out suddenly, causing everything in the apartment to go dark. A drawer slid open, and I heard Carol Lynne rifling through it. The scrape of a lighter was followed by the warm glow of a flame. Carol Lynne held it to the wick of a candle until it caught. She quickly set the candle in the candleholder on the side table and lit a few more, placing them around her apartment.

Someone knocked on the door, and she went to check out who it was. A beam of light illuminated the hallway when she opened it. "Hey, I don't know how long this blackout will last. Do you have candles to spare?" a male voice said.

She said, "Sure," and came back in, going for the drawer where she stashed her candles. The man followed behind her and paused as we made eye contact. His hair was parted in the center and was chin length. It looked a little greasy. He was wearing all black, and his t-shirt had a band logo that said McRiff.

Keith.

He gave me a chin lift and said, "ey."

I returned his greeting in the same fashion.

When she handed over the candles, the lights came back on.

"Thanks a lot. I guess I won't need them," he said.

"No, take them. This reprieve might only be temporary."

He chuffed, "Guess you're right. That usually happens. I'm gonna have to look into stocking up on some of my own." He took them, thanked her, and left.

The clock that hung high on the opposite wall said that it was 7:30. A chill ran down my spine. "Damn! The time."

I shoveled the chili in my mouth, doing my best to ignore the burning. After helping my friend wash the dishes, I replaced the dishtowel on the oven handle and hurried to the coat closet. I grabbed my coat and bag from the hanger and slipped into my boots.

"The lights may go out again. Why don't you stay the night?" she asked.

I pulled open her front door while buttoning my coat. "I can't. Bri is coming over tomorrow. I have to go with her to a dress fitting since I missed her dress choosing party."

The door opened across the hall, and Carter stepped out. I turned back to Carol Lynne.

"Sweetie, do you really want to be stuck on the train if the power goes out again? Plus, the roads are still a mess from the snowstorm."

I took a few steps down the stairs. "I'll be fine. Gotta go. Thanks for dinner. See you Monday." Then I rushed down the stairs and through the metal doors. I stomp-walked down the street—the snow crunching with each step.

She was right. Maybe I should have called a cab because it would really blow to be stuck in the subway car while the power went out. But I couldn't let Bri down again. So I took my chances and went down the stairs to the subway, digging into my coat pocket for my MetroCard.

After swiping the card through the reader, I stepped past the turnstile. The train pulled to a stop in the station, so I ran for it, slipping through the closest set of double doors.

There were only a handful of people in the car. I walked to the middle of the car and sat by the handrail. I took out my phone to find my kindle app. The side door slid open, and someone walked up the aisle, but I didn't pay attention until he sat next to me. My head whipped to the side.

Carter.

His spiky blond hair and lean jaw gave me an unexpected tingle that I hated. Since the café incident, I'd tried to imagine him with warts all over his stupid, chiseled jaw—the handsome bastard. I got up to leave.

"I need to apologize," he said in a low, conciliatory tone.

"Save it. I don't want anything from you except for you to leave me alone," I said with as much venom as I could muster.

"I fucked up. And I'm sorry. Look-please-stay and hear me out."

If I moved to sit anywhere else, he'd follow. I pressed my lips together and settled back in my seat. "Okay...what do you have to say?"

His legs were parted, and he rested his hands on them. "When I walked into the café, I wasn't expecting you."

What the hell did that mean? We'd texted, and he'd seen my picture before we'd agreed to go on the meetup. I made a face, and he chuckled.

"No, I mean - from what Keith told me - I was expecting..." He struggled for the words. "Someone lookin' for a hookup. Not a nice lady like yourself."

It took a second for his words to sink in. Well, now. What the hell could I say to that?

"I broke up with my girl a few months before we met," he said.

Was that the same lady I saw him with earlier today? That was probably why she gave me the death stare.

"It was a fucked-up relationship. She messed with my head, and it took a while to get away from her. Keith talked me into going on random hookups but not getting involved with anyone. So when we met at the café, I thought you were there to get some play. But then you didn't look like the type to be into that. And...I panicked. I'd only fuck up your life if we got involved... so...I left."

"You ran like a bitch! You could have just told me you weren't interested, and I would have understood."

His mouth fell open before he quickly closed it.

"Carter, I went out with some serious weirdos. One

guy was really in love with his pet tarantulas, and I wanted to run out too. But I didn't. Know why?"

Well, not entirely true. I faked a headache and left. But hey, that was still not the same as upping and leaving someone without an explanation.

With a wrinkled forehead and quirked lips, he answered, "No."

"I see things through. It would have been rude to just leave. And because I am NOT a bitch."

"You're right. Woulda been rude to walk out on him. But don't underestimate the power of panic. And my name isn't Carter. It's Reese. Reese Malone. Carter is my middle name."

My eyes moved up to the overhead posters that advertised dentists and English as a second language programs. I shut my eyes. *Wow.* I felt like a damn fool. He'd been playing me from the very beginning.

"Why are you even here?" I said after a while.

"Because I want to say sorry. And I heard you arguing with your friend about leaving."

"Why are you even bothering? Aren't we past apologies?"

The white blur outside the window slowed into solid tiles with the name of my stop. "Okay, you've said what you had to. Now we don't have to speak any further." I got up and stood by the doors, waiting for them to open when the train stopped moving.

"Wait." He got up to walk out with me.

I groaned.

"You told me what you had to. Now please leave me alone and stop following me." Even though this guy was aggravating, deep down, I knew that I was safe with him. Maybe it was because he'd rejected me so thoroughly before, that I felt like no harm would come to me. At least physically, anyway.

The doors opened, and I shot out of the car.

"I'm not following you; I'm walking beside you." He smirked like he thought he was cute.

I rolled my eyes.

Seriously?!

"What. Is. Your. Problem?!" I growled as we walked up a set of staircases to the street level. He walked with his hands in his jacket pockets while I huddled in my jacket with my arms wrapped around me.

"No problem." His smirk turned into a genuine smile. "I just figured I owed you an apology and safety."

What?

"Safety?" I asked.

"Yeah. It's late, and you shouldn't be walking alone in NYC at night. Especially when a blackout is possible. And...I felt bad that I left you during a storm. That's not something I usually do, and it's been bugging me. I worried after I left that you got home okay."

Well, at least he had a conscience and wasn't a complete dick.

"Thanks," I said stiffly, which made him laugh. Its deep timber coiled around my stomach, and a begrudging smile broke out on my face. *Ugh*..the idiot.

"Keith told me you were a chef."

"No. I studied culinary arts, but I'm not a cook. Far from actually." Why would Carol Lynne say that? I bet it was because she thought it was more appealing.

"No kidding? What do you do?"

"A secretary."

He nodded. "So, you studied culinary arts? You wanted to work in a restaurant?"

"Yes...things didn't turn out that way." I swallowed past the tightness in my throat. "What about you?"

His eyes narrowed, then smoothed out again. "I own a catering company, but I'm a delivery guy, so it's off to the races, most days," he shared. "You a secretary? Where?"

"A PR firm."

His brows hiked. "That's a far step away from cookery."

Cookery? I giggled, and his lips curved attractively

in a smile. I had to turn away because it was so sexy, I could stare at it for a long time.

I stopped walking in front of a little door beside a convenience store.

"Well, this is me." It was weird that he now knew where I lived. But he didn't strike me as the stalker type, so I guess it was okay.

Reese said, "It was nice talking to you," while subtly taking in his surroundings.

"Thanks for walking me home."

He winked at me, and I swear, butterflies fluttered in my stomach.

With a quick chin lift, he said, "take care." He was backing away.

I smiled politely at him and said, "You too."

I dug the keys out of my pocket and unlocked the door. When I turned back, Carter...Reese had already made it halfway down the block, blending in with the pedestrians who were trudging down the snowy side-walk. I went in, closed the door, then made my way up to my apartment, relieved that I'd made it home safe.

CHAPTER 3

REESE

*R*eese carried tray stacks to the back of his truck while Dave carried a silver coffee earn and empty white coffee cups.

A man whose bald head glinted from the sun approached Reese. The FBI ID tag that was pinned to his suit made Reese pause.

"Excuse me. You, Malone?" the man asked. The reflection that came off of his eyeglasses obscured his eyes.

"Yeah," Reese responded.

"I'm Agent Smalls, an investigator for the FBI. I need to ask you some questions about someone you're associated with."

Reese turned to his Steve, "Finish up for me, bro. I'll be back in a second."

Dave nodded and left.

Agent Smalls led Reese a bit away from the truck and asked, "Do you know somebody by the name of Frank Cantelli, he goes by Frankie Fish."

"Yeah, I know him," Reese answered and crossed his arms.

"What do you know about him?" The agent asked as he rested both fists on his hips.

"Uncle to my ex. He's a made man from what I could tell."

"From what you could tell? So you're sayin' that you were never involved with him?"

Reese shook his head and looked off in the distance. "Naw. He was busy doin' his thing, and I was busy doin' mine."

"Except...he's interested in your thing now?" Agent Smalls asked.

Reese looked at the man and nodded. "My ex suddenly took an interest."

Smalls tilted his head, "Good. Keep her interest. We need to know where they're funneling their money to."

Reese shook his head. "No. I don't wanna get involved with them. Can't you send investigators to figure this out?"

One side of Smalls' mouth twitched. "We have our way of doing things, Malone. This is the best route to get to what we need for the bust." Smalls reached in his back pocket and pulled out his wallet. He grabbed a small white card from the side pocket and handed it to Reese. Then said, "That's my number. I already have yours and I'll be in touch."

CHAPTER 4
SARAH

The bling from Brianne's wedding dress shimmered and reflected light on the walls of the elegant pink dressing room. My beautiful, statuesque sister inspected the fit of her gown in the full-length mirror. She resembled a runway model. At least that's what people said to her when they came up to her on the street.

Her dress was form-fitting with a sweetheart neckline—the mermaid gown with lace detail overlay flowed down into a gorgeous lace train.

I huddled in the corner with my arms and legs crossed. "You're glowing, Bri. Troy will flip when he sees you."

She wore a worried expression. "Do you think so? I love it, but I don't know if he will."

"Why would you think that?"

"He's been hypercritical lately. Something at work has got him down because it's unlike him. I keep asking if he really wants to marry me, and he says yes. He acts like I'm crazy for even asking."

Jeez.

"Are you sure that *you* want to do this?"

"Of course. I'm crazy about Troy, and I know he feels the same about me. Maybe it's wedding stress added to work stress."

Hmm, I wasn't entirely convinced, but as long as she was, that's all that mattered. Time to move this conversation to safer territory. "Remember when we were kids, and I used to dress like you?"

"And you annoyed the crap out of me because you were forever stealing my lip gloss and wearing my crop tops and cargos. I couldn't wear anything I wanted because it was always in the hamper. Yes, I remember."

Wow, she had total recall and apparently still felt some kinda way. She used to complain about her clothes going missing.

Looking back, I could understand how that would be annoying. "I wish I was here to help you choose your dress. Who knows your style better than me? Since I wore it regularly."

She giggled. "I've moved on from velour tracksuits and hoop earrings, but I get you."

"How was Mom? Did you eventually choose the dress she liked or did you go on your own?"

She shot me a 'you have no idea' expression, which sparked my curiosity.

"I got to choose the dress, so long as she chose the veil," she admitted.

I threw my head back and laughed.

Her reflection's mouth dropped. She spun around and gaped at me.

"What?" I asked as my laughter cleared.

"Nothing. Seeing you laugh is...different."

I rolled my eyes and got back to our previous subject. "Your law school skills must have come in handy," I said.

She wrinkled her nose. "She accused me of being just like Dad after I got my way."

I shook my head. Leave it to Mom to act like the injured party.

"What about you, huh?" she asked as she resumed examining the fit of the back of her dress in the angled mirrors. "When are you going to date again? I understand that you don't want to talk about it, but you have to move on."

My heart sputtered, causing my chest to heave.

Oh hell, not this again. This was a no-go subject with me, and my family knew it. My heart picked up speed.

"Start cooking again. Start doing the things you love and stop blaming yourself for what happened to Jason and Daphne. None of that was your fault."

"I'm not blaming myself." My protests were point-less because they knew I'd devoted years to living in my shell.

"Yes, you are." Her tone gentled. "We see it every time we ask what you've been up to, and all you talk about is TV." She stopped inspecting her back and pinned me with her gaze to give emphasis to her point.

I heaved to get a handle on my breathing.

This room was small. Too small. My breathing increased in speed, and I tried to fight it as my vision swam.

Bri turned around. "Sarah?" Her voice was filled with concern, but I ignored her.

Air. I needed out! I shot up and ran out of the room, past the rack of dresses and scattered shoppers, and up the stairs to street level. Finally, I threw the double glass door open that led out to the sidewalk.

The side of the building cooled the back of my legs and I hunched over. The pavement was blurry while I heaved air in my lungs.

A few minutes later, Bri showed up wearing the pink silk robe that the shop provided her. "I'm so sorry, Essie. I didn't mean to upset you." She wrapped her arms around me and held me close. Maybe it was because Bri was there for me or because I couldn't avoid the pain. Perhaps a bit of both. I let go and cried...hard. My body trembled. She held onto me, rested her head on top of mine, and cried. She said, "Sorry."

It took a while for me to calm down and regain my breath. The cool air revitalized my lungs. "I'm sorry too, for not being there for you in the first place. For messing up. For everything. But please...please don't bring up Jason and Daphne."

Her forehead wrinkled. "Sorry. I didn't know that you'd react this way, or else I wouldn't have said anything."

"Please stop telling me what I should and shouldn't do with my life. I'll live at my own pace."

The light dawned in her eyes. "Essie, you should talk to someone. A therapist or someone to get closure. It's not okay that normal life situations set you off."

People stared as they passed by. The cool weather

finally made me feel cold. I took her hand. "Let's go inside and finish your fitting."

The next evening, while on my couch, I aimed the remote at the TV and hit the power button. The illumination of the screen made me unclenched my jaw for the first time today as I navigated to *Wheel*. The flickering lights of the spinning wheel settled my stomach.

I was definitely going to call Carol Lynne about the pie offer. Lord knew I had barista skills to include on my resume.

I ran my fingers across the edge of the microwaved mac and cheese tray that sat on my coffee table to check if it was cool enough to eat.

As I moved the cheesy pasta around with a fork, my phone on the side table rang. I abandoned the meal to answer it. The name on the display made me smile. "Hey, Dad. How are you?"

"Alright. My cholesterol is a bit high, so the doctor said I needed to cut down on salt. But I'm going to hang on to the word 'down' and not out."

His lawyer's mind fixated on jargon. But, in this case, it wasn't to his benefit. "Dad. Come on. Be healthy. Bri's getting married, and she may have kids.

You want to stick around to meet your grandchildren, don't you?" I hope he caught on to the seriousness of my tone while I stared at my dinner and shoved the guilt aside.

"I would love that, and you know it. But that's not why I called. I'd like to know how you're doing, kid." I loved when he referred to me like that. He'd been calling me kiddo since I was little. It morphed into 'kid,' and that became my special name. Bri was princess, and Charlie was just Charlie.

"I'm okay, Dad." Bri must have spilled about my meltdown. "Bri and I had a moment while she was at her fitting. Better now after a good cry session." I sensed the reluctance in his sigh.

"She's worried that you won't be able to stand at the altar at the wedding."

"What are you saying? She's uninviting me?"

"She thinks it's best if you sit with the guests while the ceremony goes on. You'll still be there, but not standing up with the rest of them."

"I—" What? My mind raced, replaying the events of yesterday, trying to work out what I did that was so bad that she would really be so mean. "This was because I cried, wasn't it? What's the worst that could happen? That I'll cry at the ceremony? Big deal! People do that at weddings! It's not like I'll stand out."

He drew in a breath. "Your sister said that you're still deeply affected by...your loss, and you may not be able to handle it. She's worried about you, kid. She's afraid that it might scare you."

My ass! She didn't want me to be up there crying because it would take the attention off of her. Everyone in our family knew what happened, and they'd be watching to see if I was still a basket case. Hurt and shame radiated through my body. "Fine, Dad. I won't show. If it'll make things easier for her." I wanted to hang up but couldn't because I was speaking to my father.

"Oh no, she wants you to be there—"

"Just not be seen," I interrupted.

He sputtered.

I could imagine her convincing him that this was for the best. He'd probably objected. She would have insisted, and he'd agreed to talk to me to smooth things over so that her dumb idea would be more palatable.

"I'll talk some more to your sister," Dad said.

"No need, Dad. It's fine." My voice was tight. Plus, I don't want to stress him out by forcing him in the middle. Making him choose between his daughters wasn't cool.

"I'll talk to her. Then we'll see." After we said our

goodbyes and hung up, I sat on my couch with my elbow bent and my head resting on my fisted hand. I stared at the television without paying attention to the show. I was too pissed off to cry.

She'd seen me with my guard down, and she'd kicked me out of her wedding party because of it. I would have never done anything like that to her. It would serve her right if I didn't go at all, and she'd be left explaining why I wasn't there to our relatives.

But then again, she'd make up an excuse that I was sick or depressed. Lord knew my family believed me to be a grieving widow who had never recovered. She could say *anything* about me, and they'd believe it. So either I stayed away from her wedding, or I sucked it up for a day.

Not that I felt like going anymore. I wouldn't have the strength to pretend all day in front of my family. Then again, this was my sister. Sigh.

The wedding wasn't until June. I could decide then. Picking up my tray from the coffee table, I finished my dinner.

CHAPTER 5

I was just about to leave Carol Lynne's after unloading my family drama when the door opened across the hall and Carter...Reese...whatever, walked out. His brows quirked up when our eyes locked.

He turned to Keith and said, "See ya next week, bro. And don't get into too much fuckin' mess while I'm gone."

Keith grunted in acknowledgment, and they did that boy hand-clapping thing.

I went down the stairs, pushed through the metal door and opened my umbrella as fast as possible once outside. The wet smell of concrete was a familiar scent, as spring was upon us. The journey home would be safe tonight. Downpours deterred bad guys, or at least that was my current theory.

"Yo Sarah, wait up!"

Someone called out from behind as I power walked down the street. I slowed my walk while glancing over my shoulder. A guy in a gray hoodie jogged towards me.

I stopped breathing, and my heart jumped in my throat. After a few seconds passed by, I recognized who it was and let go of my breath.

"Damn girl, where's the fire?" Reese slowed his jog when he caught up.

"Sorry, I don't like to be out at night. Especially rainy ones."

He took the umbrella to shield both of us. I huddled closer to him, not having much of a choice. His enormous body hogged most of the space, causing the rain to wet my shoulder.

After rehashing Bri's drama with Carol Lynne, I wasn't in the mood to make conversation with anyone, much less the guy who'd walked out on me. Thankfully, the station wasn't that far.

"Then why are you out in the first place?"

"Family drama. I needed to talk to my friend."

"Hmm. I feel you. Got enough of that to deal with."
As we descended the stairs of the subway station, the
stink of metal filled my nostrils. He closed my umbrella
and handed it back. We swiped our metro cards,
pushed through the turnstile and walked down a set of
stairs to the platform.

Noticing his street lingo, I asked a common question, "where are you from?"

He lowered his hood, revealing his blond hair and
lean jawline. Running his fingers along the top of his
head, he answered, "Here. New York."

His fingers were so masculine. My heart gave a
slight thump that I shoved aside and focused on our
conversation. "I'm from here too. Just meant, which
borough are you from?"

"Brooklyn. You?"

"The city. Midtown."

He whistled. "You must come from serious cake
then, huh?"

I wrinkled my nose, not liking how that question
made me feel. "Just my dad. I work as a secretary."

"Yeah, at a PR firm. You told me already."

Wow. He remembered? I scanned my brain to recall
something he shared. "You're a caterer, right?"

"I own the company, yeah. But I deliver the food we

cater to the customers. Chris, our food director, plans the menu and supervises cooking... I like to move around a lot, not being in the same place every day, so I stayed in delivery."

"So you come from cake too, literally."

He let out a chuckle, which caused the butterflies I didn't know were there to flutter. "Cute. I gotta remember to tell Steve that one."

"Who's Steve?" I asked.

"He's the guy I deliver food with." He wanted to say something but held his tongue.

The rumble of our train's approach made us stop talking. We both backed away from the edge as it thundered past us, causing my hair to blow and the platform to vibrate.

The doors opened to a packed train. Reese stood next to the doors, with another person standing next to him, so there was no room for me. Every available rail was taken. My breathing escalated as the doors closed and the train rolled forward.

An arm wrapped around my waist and yanked. I came up against a hard body. I turned in Reese's arms, and his eyes roamed my face while his arms held me like a band. His face was smooth with light, blond stubble. There was a scar on his right brow where hair was absent. He was the kind of man who lit me up on the inside. If I gave him a chance, he'd light my heart on fire.

Reese rubbed little circles along my back. I closed my eyes and let the feel of his palm steady my nerves. Two stops later, it was my turn to get off. He grabbed my hand and led me off the train. After we were walking on the platform, I tugged on my hand, but he only tightened his grip.

As we made our way up to the street, he let go of my hand, took my umbrella, opened it and shielded us both. Resting his hand on my shoulder, he said, "I could get used to taking the train, but next time, we'll take my truck."

"Next time?" What was he talking about?

"Next time you're at your girl's. We'll take my truck."

"Listen. Thank you for walking me home, but you don't have to go out of your way."

"No trouble, babe. I don't mind."

I swallowed. "I saw you with that girl in the store the other day. I don't want to get involved in drama."

He pulled us to a stop. "That was my ex, Gina. Ex as in ex. Done. Don't want to go there anymore."

My face went cold at the memory of her death

stare. "Then why did she look at me like she wanted to kill me?"

"She thinks I belong to her, so if anyone looks in my direction, she gets pissed. I can't even tell you how many times I've had to pull her off someone."

Jeez.

"Why would you think that I would want to get into a fight with her? I spent most of the past few years living in my own hell. I don't want to jump into your problems."

He whipped his head away for a second before turning his head back. "Good point. But I want to be happy too. I want a chance at something good. I don't want my ex controlling my life."

His tone had a ring of sadness that squeezed my heart. But that small, sensible voice in the back of my mind warned me to be careful.

We walked the rest of the way in silence. While we were at my door, he handed me back my umbrella, pulled up his hood and walked away.

I fiddled with the lock until it opened and trudged up to my apartment.

After washing up, I changed into some pale blue sleep shorts and a matching cami. Then I curled up on the couch and turned on the TV. While I was staring vacantly at the screen, my phone buzzed.

Ray Stevenson: Setting up dinner with you, Charlie and Bri @ my place. It's been a while since the 4 of us shared a meal.

Sigh. This again.

CHAPTER 6

"Glad you made it, kid." Dad kissed the top of my head. "Come in. Your brother and sister are already inside."

I owed this to Dad.

After hanging up my jacket on the coat rack, I took a deep breath and walked down the hall into the living room. Bri and Charlie sat on the couch in the living room, talking.

Seeing them huddled together made me want to do an about-face. Being the odd man out in our family was the norm. Nothing had changed since we were kids, and I suspected nothing ever would.

Charlie stood up and wrapped me up in a hug. I pasted a smile on my face and returned his hug. Bri's smile was tight as we moved in for an embrace. At least I wasn't the only one who was uncomfortable about this.

Our dad walked in from the hall, distracted by the text he was sending. After he was done, he announced, "Dinner is in the dining room."

I strode into the dining room, eager to get this over with. The room hadn't changed much since we'd lived here.

Dad wasn't a fan of change, so he hadn't redecorated. The same school and vacation pictures that had hung on the wall when we were kids were still there. Not to mention all of his knick-knacks.

There was a new photo, though. In it, Dad was with an older blond lady, his girlfriend, Connie. We hadn't met, but he mentioned her sometimes. In the photo, they were standing on an elevated platform with the city of Paris sprawled behind them. It looked like a selfie that had been blown up and printed.

We sat in the same places that we'd occupied growing up. Mine was by the sideboard along the wall near Dad, who sat at the head. Charlie sat opposite me, and Bri sat next to him.

The table and chairs were an ornate cherry wood. The seats were padded in a striped satin, off-white material. When Dad said that he was "redecorating," it meant that the batting and fabric on the dining room chairs were being changed. That was the awesome thing about coming here. It was home, and was more comforting than my musty, dorm room-sized apartment.

A tray of baked ziti was at the center of the table. Our favorite cola drinks and freshly baked garlic bread were by our places. Dad must have ordered from the Italian restaurant downstairs. I forgot my trepidation for a second and felt a thrill of anticipation as I took in the delicious food that sat in front of me.

My sister whined. "Daddy, you know I can't eat this. I have a wedding dress I need to fit into."

I fought the urge to roll my eyes, scratching my nose to hide the face I was making. Seriously.

"Not even a little? Have a small bite, nothing much." Dad coaxed her like he had when we were teenagers, and he'd had to talk her into eating.

"Can't we just skip to what you wanted to say?" My sister was losing patience.

"Brianne." His voice held the edge that a parent's would when they were about to discipline their child.

She must have sensed it, too, because she pouted as she picked up her fork.

Charlie and I picked up ours and dug in.

Dad speared ziti with his fork before popping it in

his mouth. "What I wanted to talk to you kids about is the wedding." He swallowed and sipped his cola. "Brianne, it's not right that you appointed your sister a bridesmaid and now you're taking it away."

There was something about what he said that made me feel weird. Like I was a child being mistreated, and he was settling the dispute as a parent.

I didn't want to be a part of her wedding if she didn't *want* me there. I didn't want him to force her into tolerating me. That's what she'd be doing if he made her change her mind.

Before he could say more, I interrupted. "Dad, wait. I'm okay with sitting it out. It's her day, and if that's what she wants, then that's what she wants. I'm okay with it." I didn't add that I was going to be the bigger person by attending.

Dad set serious eyes on me. "What will the family think if you're not up there? They'll think there was something wrong between you and your sister."

There *was* something wrong. But I didn't voice that out loud.

He turned his attention to Bri. "The family will ask questions, and it'll make for an uncomfortable experience."

"Really, Dad. It's okay. I understand that she's uncomfortable with me and my panic attacks. It's okay,

I promise. Besides, who'll know about this? No one will know that I was a part of the bridal party."

He ignored me and stared at Bri. "I'm not saying that you have to come to a decision right now, Brianne," Dad continued like I'd said nothing. Gah! I hated when he did that. "Just think about it, okay? I don't want you to do anything that you'll end up regretting."

Bri stared at her food. Her forehead was wrinkled.

I hated this. I seriously *hated* it. Being made to feel like I was an obligation sucked. Despite what everyone thought, I had some pride.

"Dad. Please. I'm serious. It's okay. It truly is."

He picked up his fork to continue eating, ignoring me. This dinner wasn't going the way he intended, and I felt terrible that he'd put so much effort into it.

We finished our meal in uncomfortable silence then hauled ass to leave.

CHAPTER 7

*S*cattered balls of crumpled-up papers were lying around my desk when I walked into the office. Didn't Brandy ever tire of acting like a child? If she had hobbies, she wouldn't have time to be evil.

I fished the phone out of my pocket and snapped a photo to save for later. Then I unfurled one of the balls to discover they were contracts that needed to be faxed this morning. I snapped another photo and spent the rest of my morning getting papers as straight as possible before faxing them.

Gerald set his coat on his chair's backrest, opened his bottom drawer, and placed his messenger bag inside before closing it. He surveyed the mess while finger-combing his combover. "She's at it already?"

"Probably happened after we left last Friday," I said.

He shook his head and took a seat. "More trips to HR? Or are you going straight to Larry Higgins?"

"I don't know if I want Larry involved. Cause if he knows, so will my father."

"Personally, if I had that ammo, I'd use it," he said as he read through a stack of papers on his desk.

I threw a smile over my shoulder even though he had his back to me. "You enjoyed your weekend?"

"I played a campaign all weekend and leveled up to the eighth wizard. So I celebrated by going out to dinner last night."

"Awesome," I said, even though I had no idea what he meant.

"What about you?"

"My sister uninvited me to be a part of her wedding party, so our dad hosted the most awkward family dinner to mend fences."

He turned and made a face. "Damn. I would rather have my weekend. No drama, except the ones from my game. Oh, by the way, about Morris's retirement party. Can you make sure there's chocolate cake?"

I chuckled. "Sure. I'll only entertain menus that offer chocolate cake."

After I sent the faxes, I made my way down to HR

for what was becoming my daily ritual. I should talk to Larry, like Gerald suggested. He was the only one who knew that my dad and the CEO were friends, and Dad was the one who got me this job in the first place.

When I returned to my desk, I leafed through a few catering menus. I passed one of them that offered a chocolate cake for dessert to Gerald for his approval.

"Lemon squares," was whispered as Matt Simms walked by.

Gerald shook his head like he thought Matt was crazy for even suggesting that idea. "Chocolate cake is the crowd favorite." His tone was no-nonsense.

"Could we get both?" I pleaded, because the idea of disappointing people when it came to food bothered me.

Gerald's lips were flat as he lowered his chin and shot me a severe stare over the rim of his glasses. Okay. Don't mess with the eighth-level wizard and his love for chocolate cake.

I was watching *Wheel* while eating microwaved chicken casserole for dinner when my phone buzzed.

Brianne: Can you call me sometime?

I deliberated for a second before going through my contacts for her name and tapping the call button.

"Es? Hey." Muffled horns and screeching brakes came through the phone.

"Bri. Where are you? Is everything okay?"

"Yes. Everything's fine. I'm driving home, actually. I called to talk about the wedding. I've been thinking about what can be done to help you out. Sorry about the way I handled everything. It worried me that my wedding will mess with you, ya know? Just like seeing me in my wedding dress messed with you when we were at the boutique."

That made me pause, because she had a point. Was I going to lose it standing at the altar? It wouldn't be fair to her.

"Hello?" she prompted.

"Yeah, I'm here. And I understand where you're coming from." I massaged my forehead.

She let out a sigh.

"What do you suggest?" I asked.

"How about we see how rehearsal goes? If it gets to be too much, you can sit it out. How does that sound?"

"Sounds fair." I'd done considerable damage to my siblings' faith in me when I'd checked out for so long. And I suppose these were the repercussions.

I forked some casserole and placed a bit in my mouth. The creamy yumminess was a welcome distraction.

"Hey listen, how about you and me meet for lunch or something before the rehearsal? We should catch up. Maybe we can have lunch or dinner. What do you think?" my sister asked.

An olive branch? "Okay." My voice was hesitant. "When?"

"I'll check my calendar and get back to you since things have been hectic lately."

"Okay, see what you have open."

We said our goodbyes and hung up. I wouldn't hold my breath that lunch would happen, especially since we're a month and a half away from the wedding. After all, Bri said it herself that she had a million things to do. But at least her heart was in the right place.

At least that didn't go as wrong as it could have. I downed the rest of my dinner.

CHAPTER 8

*C*arol Lynne and I were standing on the lunch line and I was holding a plastic container filled with salad and a bottle of water. The café downstairs was more crowded than usual, which probably had to do with the rainy weather. "She suspects that I'm working on a special project. It's like she's a dog that can sniff out other people's business." Carol Lynne unloaded her office drama to me.

"As long as she can't get her hands on it. You did the right thing hiding it the way you have."

"What about you?"

"Found contracts I was supposed to fax crumpled on the floor."

She shook her head and rolled her eyes. "It's like we have to contend with ten-year-old mean girls."

I laughed because that was exactly what it felt like.

Carol Lynne's body jolted, and she turned around, fastening her attention on the order board. "So, any news with Bri's wedding?" she whispered.

What was that about? My friend probably felt weird talking about office gossip when our coworkers were nearby.

I lowered my voice and answered, "She called me last night and offered to meet up for lunch."

"How do you feel about that?"

I pursed my lower lip. Good question. "I don't know how to feel. I'm numb to it all, so whatever happens, happens."

"Did you give more thought to the pie offer?"

What was up with her? From one question to the next. She was never this chatty after she vented about her nemesis. She was usually in her head, probably hammering out another business idea during those times.

I shrugged and answered, "Yeah, sometimes when I'm having a crappy day. Like today."

Her eyes lid up. "Idea! I'll come over and sample that pie again. We can make a list of potential distributors."

"You just came up with that?" Because that was impressive.

"Nope. I've been thinking about it for a while and lying in wait until I could spring it on you."

I laughed at the image of a cat staring at her prey in my head. We made our way to the counter and paid for our salads, and I added a bag of cookies.

When I turned around to leave, Reese was standing in line, talking and laughing with another guy.

Well, that explained why Carol Lynne was abnormally chatty.

The other guy saw me staring at Reese and said something to him. Reese's eyes searched until they found me. The corner of his left eye twitched, then he said something to his friend. The friend nodded and gave me a smirk that made me uncomfortable.

Carol Lynne towed me towards the double doors, where we exited the café. We made our way back into our building, and took the elevator upstairs into the lunchroom. There were a few people scattered about sitting at the round tables.

We took our seats, side by side, at the table in the corner. We opened the white plastic bag filled with our salads and a brown paper bag filled with bite-sized cookies.

Carol Lynne speared a few pieces of romaine and

popped them in her mouth. Then she got out her phone and started swiping away. "How about this weekend? We can shop some pies around?"

All enthusiasm for the pie offer had seeped out of me. I stared at the bag of bite-sized cookies while eating my salad and shrugged. "I guess."

"Lemme guess. Your mopiness has something to do with a handsome blond."

"I don't know what he said to the guy to make the guy smirk. Was he saying crap?"

"You like him," she accused.

I pinned my gaze to my salad, losing my appetite by the second. "Doesn't matter how I feel. It'll never happen between us. I'll stop going to that café because I can't stand seeing him."

She shook her head and sighed, "Alright. There are a million other cafés we can go to. Now. About the weekend pie thing. We can run test products."

"It'll never sell." I said with the enthusiasm of Eeyore.

She tilted her head and narrowed her eyes.

I explained, "Who's gonna buy from me? It's not like I have a kitchen that I bake out of." I answered the question she was thinking but didn't ask.

"We'll do some research about fulfilling that market."

"How am I going to bake pies and hold down a full-time job?" I countered.

She chewed her food and opened the cap on her bottle of water. After taking a swig, she asked, "How about only offering a weekend deal? Then it won't be too much of a commitment to fulfill orders in the beginning."

That didn't sound too bad. Or too risky. I gave my friend a closed-mouthed smile and nodded.

After we were done, Carol Lynne left to head back to her desk. I stayed behind to make a coffee for myself before heading back.

"So, you have the actual ability to make coffee."

I jumped, then cringed as I figured who'd said that. When I turned to give Brandy a dirty look, she was already smirking. I balled my fists.

"Make sure you get me coffee, pronto." She walked away.

Did she come all the way here just to harass me? How did she even know I was down here? Everyone had already left the lunchroom a few minutes ago.

Oh well.

I made Brandy's coffee, which was actually tea, and brought it to her. When I was down the hall on my way back to my desk, my supervisor, Max Richmond, placed something on my desk and walked away.

A Post-it note stuck to the keyboard that requested me to report to his office at my earliest convenience.

My stomach tightened.

I walked down the hall across from my cubicle to his office. Hopefully, this had something to do with the retirement party I was planning for Simms. I knocked on Richmond's door.

"Come in," his gruff voice called out.

I poked my head in. "You wanted to see me, sir?"

"Come in, close the door and have a seat."

The hairs on my arms stood up as I did as he asked.

He was a slim, balding man with brown hair and glasses. It was probably because he wore suspenders, but his shoulders came up and he reminded me of a crab. "I received a call from our client that the contract wasn't legible. They sent me a copy of the fax. What happened?"

I swallowed. "When I came in on Monday, I found balled-up pieces of paper around my desk. After I uncrumpled it, I found that it was the contracts I had to fax. So I tried to fix it and fax them, anyway. After that, I filed a complaint with HR about it."

He looked at me like I was a moron. "If there's a problem with contracts, then you come to me. You don't fix it yourself."

"I'm sorry, sir."

"Your pay will be docked because of this mistake."

What?! My eyes bulged and my mouth fell open. How the hell was that fair?

"Because of you, our company looks like we don't value our clients."

My nose stung, and I fought against tearing up because I didn't want him to see them.

"You may leave."

My chin dipped in a nod, and I got up and left.

After returning to my desk, Gerald asked, "What was that about?"

"Richmond docked my pay because the contracts I faxed were too illegible for them to sign."

He winced, then shrugged. "You know my suggestion."

Yeah. I did, but my pride hurt just thinking about going to Larry Higgins and complaining. I couldn't have my dad or my dad's friends pull me out of trouble every time.

I could feel a headache coming.

Oblivious to my pain, he asked, "Did you get that chocolate cake situation figured out?"

"No. I'll call them." At least I could make someone happy today.

I was eating microwaved chili mac while venting to Carol Lynne on speakerphone. *Jeopardy* was barely audible in the background. The rain was really pouring outside, causing us to raise our voices over it.

"Operation Pie Business will give you something to look forward to. It'll help you get your power back," my friend said. It sounded like she was having dinner as well.

That idea made me feel better. "When do you think we should start?"

"Can you bake a little in the next few days?"

"You think we can have everything ready by then?" Because that was a little too fast.

"All we need is product and business cards. Maybe a point-of-sale ad or something. I could design something for you in a jiff," she said.

"How about we wait before jumping into this? I need time. My life is changing so fast. I wish I could teleport to before all this crap started happening. I'd be content."

She sighed. "We need to act quickly."

"We need to act smart. I don't want to get in over my head."

"Okay. More research won't hurt...I guess." She sounded like someone stole her chakra beads.

I closed my eyes. "Thank you."

"What are the next steps you feel comfortable with?"

Did crawling under the blanket count? "I don't know. Baking. I can start with baking a few pie formats."

"What kind of pie formats?" my friend asked.

"Full pies and tarts. Like Pop Tarts."

"Pop Tarts...genius. How did you come up with that idea?"

"At school. We had to come up with different formats of the same dish. Like, cake and cupcakes, wraps and sandwiches. Sometimes if one version doesn't work, another will."

"Then do that. I volunteer for taste testing," she said with enthusiasm.

A small giggle popped out of me, making me feel a tiny bit better.

CHAPTER 9

"The caterer canceled and I don't know where to find another one. It has me so stressed, I'm thinking of setting up take-out and calling it done," Bri said as she sat opposite, spearing her garden salad.

The whoosh of the cappuccino machine pulled my attention to the front of the café. The blueberry muffins in the display case called to my tastebuds.

"Es?" She followed the path of my stare and shook her head.

"Sorry. Those muffins looked good."

"How you've stayed slim is beyond me, with your monster appetite."

Backhanded compliment, but eh, that was Bri. "Thanks, I guess." I shrugged.

Of all the people I'd ever met, Bri was the most beautiful. The most perfect. Her thinking that she wasn't meant there was no hope for us lesser mortals.

It made me pity her.

"Actually, I think I can help." I hesitated. "If you want. I'm planning a retirement party for a guy at work." I pulled out my phone, opened my contacts, scrolled, locating the catering company, and handed it to her. "Good rates and variety. They probably offer a wedding package."

Bri got hers out and copied the number in. "Okay, thanks. This may help. So. How's everything going with you?"

Swallowing the bite of my ham sandwich, I answered, "Had a crap day on Friday. Bullied at work and had my pay docked because of it."

She stopped typing and focused on me. Her face went hard. "What?"

I waved her off, hoping that she wouldn't make a big deal out of it. "I'm dealing with it."

Her mouth quirked to one side. "How?"

"I'm working on a side business with Carol Lynne."

My sister handed me back my phone and put hers back in her bag. "You're planning on leaving? Cool. So tell me about this side business?" She sounded enthused.

"Baking pies."

"Food? That's great, Es. Getting back to what you love. I told you..." She stopped speaking and cringed. Probably remembering my panic attack.

"Things are still new. I'm testing recipes and formats right now, and we'll see what takes. I want to go slow so things don't get too overwhelming too quickly. But it's all going so fast. Like one minute, we were just hashing out ideas, then bam! But it gives me something to fall back on if the nonsense at work keeps up."

"Why did they dock your pay?" My sister chewed and dabbed at the corners of her mouth with her tissue.

Ugh. I didn't want to talk about it because my sister would blab to Dad.

"I found some contracts balled up around my desk. I straightened them and faxed them, anyway. The client complained to my boss." I opened my sandwich to examine the lettuce while I felt her stare. She had this way that always made me feel stupid with a look. She weaponized silence. It was her unique talent.

Bri sighed. "Did you let Dad know—"

My nostrils flared. "No! Dad had done enough. I don't want to ask more of him."

"You're the only one who he's willing to help. May as well take advantage of it."

My brows knitted together. What did that mean? "Dad helps you too, Bri. Both you and Charlie. Heck, you three are as thick as thieves."

She waved me off, and it hurt my feelings. "You should talk to Dad, Es. If they're already docking your pay, he may step in." She continued eating.

"I'll see." Meaning I wouldn't. "So are we still on for rehearsals?"

She tipped her head. "Course, Es. Do you still want to?"

No. Not after all this. The breath escaped from my lips.

But this was my sister's wedding, and I should be there, and it wasn't like we hated each other.

"I just need to make sure that you want me there. It wouldn't be right if Dad pressured you into doing something you didn't want to."

Her forehead creased, and she placed a hand on my arm. "It feels like we finally have our Essie back. I don't want my wedding to send you away again."

"I'm sorry...for leaving. Guess I take after Mom after all." My gaze went towards the muffins. The similarities between my mother and me finally came into focus, and it was disappointing.

"Don't feel too bad about it, Es. We all take after her in little ways," she said while standing up. Then she walked over to the order counter, paid, and came back carrying a white paper bag. She opened it and placed a blueberry muffin in front of me.

I beamed up at her.

Later that evening, I descended the stairs of Carol Lynne's apartment with a full stomach of empanada-style apple pie and wine.

The sound of Keith's door opening made me move faster down the stairs.

"Babe, hold up," the familiar voice called out as he said goodbye to his friend.

"Can't. I gotta get home." My words were slurred.

His footsteps moved down the stairs fast until his big body was by my side.

"Why is it you're always there every stinking time I leave," I protested.

"Been waiting for you."

What? I stopped and looked at him with my mouth open.

A smile curved his lips. The handsome bastard! On cue, like he knew what I was thinking, his smile widened. *Ugh!*

We pushed past the metal door and made it onto the street.

"So, did you think about it?"

My forehead wrinkled. "What?"

"Whether we can be friends. Last time you said you didn't know if you wanted to spend time with someone with baggage. Did you decide?"

Was he serious?

While I was looking at him like he was crazy, he said, "I brought my truck. I'll drop you home."

"That's okay. I can walk."

"Cool. Now that we got that straight. I'm parked over here." Then he grabbed my hand and towed me toward his truck. Electricity shot through my arm at his touch. He looked down at me for a beat but said nothing.

I rolled my eyes while ignoring the heat in my belly as we walked.

"So, that place that I've seen you at. You work around there or something?"

"Yes, that's the Sutter building. Well, more like our company occupies two floors in that building."

"That explains why I always see you and Carolyn

there."

"It's Carol Lynne. Two names. And how do you know her name?"

"Keith told me."

After I stepped in, he slid it closed and walked around to the other side. He got in and slipped the key into the ignition. "Got time for a coffee?"

"Sure." It popped out of my mouth before I had time to think about it.

Reese started the truck and pulled out of the parking space.

"Your parents still live here, or did they move? You said that you're from the city."

"Dad lives here still. He and mom have been divorced since I was a kid."

He glanced over at me. "My dad walked out on us when I was fifteen. I had to drop out of school to help Ma look after my little brother, Sammy, who gave up karate because we couldn't afford the fees."

That was shitty. His mom must have been so stressed. Not to mention heartbroken. And, how awesome was he to help out his mom at such a young age. Would Charlie do that if he were in that position?

"Sorry to hear that you guys went through that. Did you ever go back for your GED, or did you have to leave completely?"

"Left completely. After I got my truck license, I worked to save money to open up this business and find a partner. Been working since. Don't have any time for much else. What about you?"

"I got the job I'm working at now after college and have been working there since. Though, Carol Lynne and I have been coming up with ideas for a pie business. Lately, things aren't going well at work, and she suggested that I get out and do my own thing."

"Speaking as a person who does that, I can say that it's a good idea. But what kinda stuff is going on at work?"

"Demanding that I make coffee. Which I wouldn't object to doing; it's just how she asks. I don't know. It feels like she's punishing me. She also crumpled up contracts I needed to fax. That one actually made them dock my pay."

He glanced over at me. The streetlights moved across his strong, beautiful features set in stern lines. "Shit, babe. I would have lost it."

That's because he's the boss at his company. I'm not.

"Not sure it's worth it at this point. I'm fed up with everything, you know. I wish that things could go back to being peaceful, but I don't know how."

"If you ever need help in finding a job, I can hook

you up with one. You said that you had training in the food business. I work in food. My partner may use you in the kitchen. Wherever the heck that may be."

"What happened? You're having trouble with your kitchen?"

"Yeah. Too much competition for commissary space. We're looking into finding something more permanent. The whole thing is a pain in the ass."

"How hard is it to find a permanent kitchen in New York? You'd think with all the restaurants we have here, it would be easy."

"Only if you're using that space as a restaurant. If not, you'll need to rent a commissary. That's what most food trucks do."

Reese pulled into an empty parking spot at a café, shut off the truck, and got out. He walked around to my side and slid my door open. He helped me down, closed the door, and slipped an arm around my shoulder.

My arm moved jerkily around his waist. His lips quirked in a sensual smile.

I swear, this man. Everything about him was so gorgeous.

He pulled the door open, and we walked inside. We stared at the menu. He leaned down and whispered, "what do you want?"

My stomach quivered. I played it off like I wasn't affected, but the naughty smile on Reese's face told me he knew what he was doing.

"Ah...what do you suggest?" My voice came out high pitched.

He looked back at the menu board. "Ever tried Java the Hut?"

"No, can't say that I have. You come here often?"

"Yeah. Know just about every coffee place in town, on account of being a delivery guy. Me and Steve make it our mission to scope out unknown places."

"So is that why I've seen you at work lately?"

He looked down at me. "The first time was an accident. The second time, I was hoping to find you again."

The light dawned. "Why didn't you come over and say something?"

"You looked like you were in a hurry, and you were pissed. So I waited until there was a better time to talk to you, like after you visit your friend."

Well. That was a revelation.

"So all those times we ran into each other were on purpose?"

His smile caused the butterflies in my stomach to go haywire.

I swallowed. "Do you...do you like me?"

God. That sounded dumb. My face heated, and my eyes fell to his chest.

His steely blue eyes heated. "Babe. Look at us right now."

The arm around my shoulder flexed like he was reminding me how close we were. I smiled at him.

"Next up." The clerk's bark snapped us out of our trance.

"Two regular Java the Huts." He reached behind his back pocket and pulled out his wallet. Placing a few bills on the counter and taking his change, he slipped his wallet back in his pocket and handed me my cup.

We walked back to his truck and stepped inside. I placed my cup in the holder on the side console. He did the same, started the truck, and pulled out into traffic.

"I gotta be on the road at four tomorrow morning. We got two jobs. One in White Plains and one in the city."

My jaw dropped. "Four? My god. I don't think I could survive that."

"You get used to it. I like that I move in and out of situations. Not being stuck in the same place and not having to put up with people's bullshit is great."

I nodded. "Tell me about it."

"Offer still stands. You can come work with me.

Better looking at you all day than looking at Steve. Though I may be too distracted to work."

I pursed my lips. "Distracted?"

He glanced at me with a smile curving his lips. "You got beautiful gray eyes. Kinda stormy. And shimmering."

The butterflies went wild again.

When we pulled up in front of my door, my body felt heavy. It would have been nice if this...whatever this was could have lasted longer. "Thanks for the coffee and the ride."

After taking off my seatbelt, his hand flew under my chin and tugged, focusing my attention on him. He leaned in, and I met his sensual lips halfway. He kissed my bottom lip and checked my eyes if he was welcomed. Then he moved to deepen the kiss. He tasted like coffee. His tongue swirled inside my mouth, tasting me. It was so gentle, yet there was more to it that I couldn't name. He broke away from me and placed a quick peck on my forehead.

I got out of the truck. Somehow, I made it to my door and opened it. Reese was staring at me when I turned to see him off. My wave was small and a little dorky. There might have been a grin on his face as he looked over his shoulder and pulled into traffic.

I floated up to my apartment. *Kinda stormy and shimmering.*

CHAPTER 10

I was sitting in front of my manager, Mr. Richmond, while he examined the ruined contracts. Through the blind slits, the mirrored building across the street reflected our building. I was trying to find the office I was sitting in.

Richmond's no-nonsense tone cut through my musings. "Did you offend someone in this office?" He pushed his glasses up the bridge of his nose when he raised his head to meet my eyes.

My jaw dropped.

What the hell? How was this my fault?

"No. I've been professional with all of my colleagues."

He tilted his head and shifted his lips to the side.

His eyes came down half-lidded. "Really? Because I've been getting reports that you've been spiking coffees. Does that sound like professional behavior to you?" His nostrils flared.

I gaped at him. Were the two of them sleeping with each other or something? What reports was he getting? And why had he been receiving reports when mine went unanswered? Was she blocking them? Could that even be done?

"I...I'm bad and making coffee, sir." Okay, that was dumb, but what the hell? He was going to fire me over that?! I wasn't a barista! He was worried about coffee and not about contracts?

My fists clenched on my lap because I wanted to punch him. That sleazy bastard was probably sleeping with her. For all Brandy's evil, she was pretty, so I could see why he'd be interested.

"This is strike two, Ms. Stevenson."

I barely managed to not bare my teeth when I said, "I understand, sir." I stood up, thanked him for his time, and left before words spewed from my mouth that would get me fired.

Despite my anger, I was also relieved that he hadn't fired me right then. It meant there was still time to find a job.

Gerald, Greg, and Deb were waiting around my

desk after I got out of Richmon's office to go to the retirement party.

"What happened?" Gerald asked.

"Brandy complained to him that I didn't make her coffee properly. He told me I was behaving unprofessionally."

They wore similar expressions of confusion, but I didn't elaborate because we had somewhere to be. So I just nodded and asked, "You guys ready?"

We walked downstairs to the conference room where Simms's retirement party was being held.

People were filing into the room and going over to Matt Simms. Our group joined the crowd. The gray-haired, spectacled man said, "We're packing right now. So everything is in boxes. Hopefully, the move will go smoothly, and the truck makes it to our house in Boca."

Some people left the crowd and meandered to the table, which was filled with a variety of sandwiches, finger foods, and desserts.

A familiar, handsome blond man was setting up the dessert table, and Brandy was chatting him up. He was paying more attention to setting up the station than he was to her.

Dennis and Gerald went to the table while Deb and I were inspecting each station. Carol Lynne walked up to us. "It's Reese."

Deb's eyes bounce between the two of us. "Who's Reese?"

Carol Lynne pointed at Reese, and Deb's eyes followed until she saw him. "Oh, my god."

"Sarah's man," Carol Lynne said, probably because she didn't want Deb to get any ideas.

Deb looked at me with her eyebrows raised, then glanced back at Reese. At that moment, he looked up at us. His eyes found mine, and his lips curved into a smile. Deb nearly squealed. I smiled back at him. Carol Lynne chuckled at Deb's reaction.

Brandy looked at the group of us. She gave me stink face when we locked eyes.

Reese said something to Steve, who looked up. He smiled, and I returned a shy one. As Reese walked up to me, while Carol Lynne towed a dreamy-eyed Deb, whose eyes never left the handsome man, to the finger food station.

He bent down and planted a soft kiss on my lips, and threaded both of his hands through mine.

"Didn't know you worked in this building, babe. Nice surprise."

"Real nice," I confirmed.

"How did you know to hire my company?"

"Complete coincidence. I didn't even know the name of your company. Just knew that you guys served chocolate cake, and that was what people wanted."

Reese's chuckle was rich. He was handsome in a classic sort of way, yet he gave off a bad boy vibe. The other women in the room didn't even try to hide their stares.

"I better get back. We got a full spread, so enjoy." He kissed me again. Then he pulled away and rejoined Steve.

Brandy was standing with her hips tilted to one side and her arms folded. She redoubled her efforts by running her hand along his arm. He stopped what he was doing and said something that made her pout. Then he looked over at me and winked.

This kind of thing happened a lot with an attractive man. I'd probably have to fight off clawing women with a stick. Not something I was used to. Jason, although handsome in his own way, had been no match for Reese in the looks department.

My brain froze.

That was a mean thing to think. I shut my eyes for a beat longer than a blink to fight against the guilt that swam in my chest.

I rejoined Carol Lynne and Deb. "What are you guys having?"

"Mushroom and cheese-filled cups look good."

Deb eventually strayed off. I used the opportunity to whisper in Carol Lynne's ear. "Pie offer needs to be close to being complete. Did you set up the business cards?"

Her brown eyes rounded and her forehead puckered. "What happened?"

"I need those cards as quickly as possible. I don't even care what the name is. Just print something."

"Sarah, what happened?" Her head tilted to the side, and her voice became a little more serious.

"Not here. Just letting you know what I need."

"Did something happen?"

I clenched my jaw and tried not to raise my voice. "Look at where we're standing, Carol Lynne. We can't talk now." Wasn't that obvious?

Walking away from her, I marched over to a station and yanked a pinwheel off the table. I glanced over to Reese, who was trying to work while Deb asked him questions. She was holding up her phone and waiting. Reese said something to Steve and went back to work. Steve reached in his chef's coat pocket to give her a card.

She looked disappointed as she took it. When our eyes met, her neck got very red.

I chomped on the pinwheel, not tasting it. I could swear that snakes filled this place.

CHAPTER 11

*B*ri wore knee-length aquamarine pants and a gauzy cream top while she walked down the makeshift aisle with Dad. I was standing between Lauren, her maid of honor, and Alison, the other bridesmaid.

The trees were beautiful this time of year in Central Park. They should have had their wedding out here. The pictures would have been lovely. But she didn't want to have the possibility of it being rainy. Understandable, I guess.

Dad handed Bri off to Troy and stepped aside. Troy was wearing khaki shorts and a navy polo shirt. His hair was thinning, so he grew it long and brushed it to the front and gelled it. The most attractive feature about him was his vivid blue eyes.

"After we're married, we'll leave first, then Lauren and Patrick, followed by Es and Ryan, and Alison and Carl. We'll take pictures while everyone else goes to the reception, and that's it."

Dad checked his watch and announced. "Okay, everyone. Reservation for Stevenson at the Brahma Spice."

We were walking on the path towards the park exit when dad wrapped his arm around my shoulder. "How are you doing, kid?"

"Fine, Dad." My tone may have been a little defensive.

"Just checking, Sarah. Don't be so touchy." Dad's voice held that admonishing tone he'd taken when we were kids.

Damn. I was over-sensitive. My caring father didn't need his head bitten off because he'd asked a simple and appropriate question.

"Sorry." I wrapped both arms around him in an apologetic hug. "I'm good. How about you? Will you bring Connie to the wedding?"

"Yes, of course. She couldn't make it today because she had a last-minute change in a fundraiser that she's putting together," he answered. He wanted to ask me if I was bringing someone; I could feel the question coming off him.

It bugged me that he refrained from asking, so I answered. "I started seeing someone. His name is Reese Malone. We're new, so it didn't feel right to invite him. He's nice, and he owns a catering company. We met on a blind date."

Dad said nothing. He didn't have to because his mouth dropped open, which communicated enough.

A tiny part of me was insulted. Was it so hard to believe that someone would date me?

Stop being so defensive. He didn't mean it that way.

We made it out of the park and walked towards the corner crossing. The honking horns and engine noise generated by the multi-lane traffic prevented us from speaking until after entering the restaurant, where the others were waiting.

Dad made his way to the hostess and gave her the reservation. After scrolling through her tablet, she smiled and led us to the private room he had reserved.

The archways were a rich honey-colored wood and were cut into the Taj Mahal shape, with black flowers carved into them. Beautiful black lanterns hung from the ceiling and were scattered throughout the restaurant.

We took our seats, and I said to Dad, "This place is awesome. I've never been here before."

Charlie piped in, "You would have if you came here last year when we invited you."

Dad glared at Charlie, and Bri elbowed him.

Guess I wasn't forgiven by everyone. I stared down at my empty plate and bit my lips, and hoped they didn't tremble. I took a few cleansing breaths and admired the lanterns. Their image was swimming now. I kept to myself for the rest of the dinner.

CHAPTER 12

*M*y eyes were as glassy as my sister's, and new brother-in-law's as they danced while gazing at each other at their wedding reception. Brianne was radiant, as I knew she would be. This was harder to take than I'd thought. Not that I wasn't happy for them, because I was. The misunderstanding we'd had last month was because of her wanting to do the right thing but not going about it properly. At least, that was my current perspective.

My brother sat in the now empty seat beside me. He looked debonair in his midnight blue suit—the ass.

"You okay, Es?" he asked as he leaned in close to me.

There went my good mood. "Yeah." I turned away

and focused on the other guests. He was not forgiven for his comment yesterday.

"Sorry for what I said at the restaurant."

"Did Dad or Bri ask you to apologize? Spare me, okay?"

Charlie let out a breath and rested his hand on my forearm. He inclined his head, and raised his brow. "For real, Es."

I studied my hands. The only reason I didn't storm off was because we were sitting at the head table, and it would have caused a scene.

"Why do you even care?" I sighed. "Look, it's fine. Everything's fine, just go back to your table and leave me alone. I won't bother you if you don't bother me."

The breath he took sounded like a frustrated one. "That's not cool with me. I want to bother you." He nudged my forearm. "I'm your brother. If I can't bother you, then who's left?"

"Is that why you said what you did? Because you wanted to *bother* me? And you weren't sorry about it yesterday. It took you a day to apologize after you said it. So forgive me if I don't fall for it."

For some inconceivable reason, his lips twitched. I wanted to punch him.

"Cut me some slack, sis. Things have been crazy since yesterday, and you know it. After you left with

Dad and Connie to drive up here, I didn't get a chance to talk to you alone until now. But I'm here, and I hope that means something."

I met my brother's eyes. The sincerity of his words meant a lot. Charlie was a proud man, and he rarely apologized to anyone. So I appreciated his effort. I relaxed, tilted my head and gave him a sheepish smile. He tapped a peck on the top of my head.

"Sorry for my outburst. It was just that I already feel bad about missing out on so much. What you said nearly made me cry, and I didn't want to do it in front of Bri. She would've kicked me out of the wedding party."

My brother held me close and rocked me back and forth. That gesture communicated how sorry he was.

Our father's eagle-eyed gaze was on us, and a smile spanned his face. "Dad's happy."

Charlie turned to look at Dad. "To be honest, I'm surprised Mom and Dad aren't at each other's throats with the way Dad carried on at the office."

That perked me up. "Oh? What did he say?" This surprised me. Dad never spoke badly about Mom. Maybe he behaved differently with Charlie.

"He said that if mom flaunted her boyfriend, then he'd flaunt Connie."

I shook my head. "You would think after all this time

being divorced, they would find some way to get along, or at least be civil."

Charlie inclined his head. "Yeah. That's what happens when you still love someone but can't stand them."

"Well...at least they're behaving themselves for Bri's sake." We both looked in our mom's direction. She was at another table, talking and laughing with Aunt Clara while her date, a man who looked to be about Charlie's age, examined his fork.

A woman in a silver dress and long blond hair walked past us with eyes for Charlie. She frowned at my proximity to my brother. He excused himself and strutted his way up to her. Motioning to me, he said something. Her eyes met mine, and she laughed.

My face heated.

He led her to the dance floor.

My mom and her sisters came up to me, and I hid my eye roll. "Your Aunt Clara has someone she wants you to meet," Mom said. "She'll give you his number." Aunt Clara took out her phone. *God*. Not this again. Mom caught my eye roll.

"Come on, Essie, this will be good for you. Look at how being married has affected Brianne now that she has settled down. It's your turn."

Ugh. Kill me now.

I wavered between politely turning them down or taking the number so they would quit badgering me. The latter offered a path filled with no arguments, so I fished out my phone from my sky-blue clutch.

"There's nothing wrong with casual dating, Mom. I've been doing that lately," I muttered to myself.

Delight colored her voice. "Oh, how lovely. You're moving on again."

She heard that?

I slipped the phone back in my clutch. "If you'll excuse me...I see some people I haven't said hi to."

I shot off the chair, smiled into the distance at no one in particular, and weaved around the room until I was outside of the ballroom. Closing the French doors, I leaned against a wall and breathed in the warm evening air.

Wishing Mom and I had a closer relationship was futile. She was who she was, and no one was going to change that. After my parents' divorce, she was too busy chasing after her acting career to spend time with us. It would have been nice to do things together when we had our court-appointed visits, but she left us to our own devices.

Charlie was the first one to claim that he was too busy for visits. Bri followed next, saying that she was staying at a friend's house. That left only me for the visits, but I never tried to get out of them because I felt sorry for her. During those times, I tested recipes in her kitchen and attempted to keep her in the loop of the family's goings-on. Not that she cared.

When everything went down in my life, she wasn't there. She was probably at a cast party or something. So all that effort I'd put into our relationship clearly meant nothing.

I inhaled the clean night air while staring down at the beautiful cobblestone walkway to slow my accelerated breathing.

"Sarah?"

A man wearing a crisp white chef's coat with gray slacks and a black hooligan cap stood before me. His voice was familiar, but I couldn't place his face in the dark.

"Uh...hi," I answered.

"It's Reese," he said as he walked up to me.

"Oh. Hi. What are you doing here?"

"Workin' tonight. I take it you're one of the guests?"

"A bridesmaid, actually. This is my sister's wedding."

Reese nodded like he was impressed and came to stand closer. His face set in concern as his eyes took in my unshed tears.

"Why are you upset? Is it because the relatives are asking when it will be your turn?"

I smiled. "Something like that. How did you guess?"

"I work a lot of weddings and overhear a lot of talk."

Well, that made sense, I guessed. "My family can't accept that I don't want to get married and are forever shoving me into situations that will never work—"

"Like setting you up on dates with guys who're into tarantulas and who run out on you?" He laughed.

Wow, that was different. Most men took themselves too seriously to joke at their own expense.

"Something like that." I'm sure my expression was incredulous after he'd shown this side of himself, which was...refreshing.

"You're beautiful. Why hasn't some guy scooped you?" He changed the subject.

"I couldn't date."

"Why? A guy?"

I paused. "Two people, actually." My admission was a begrudging one.

He stood with his hands in his pocket. "Two guys, and you're ready to give up on men? Come on," he said in a good-natured, coaxing tone.

This conversation was headed down a road where I

didn't want it to go. But instead of sidestepping like I usually did, I answered for some strange reason.

"Not guys. Just one man and a baby."

All humor drained from his face, and it went hard. He narrowed his eyes. "What?"

"I dated someone throughout college. We had just graduated, were living together, and I was three months pregnant. One night, I craved ice cream and sent him out on a run. A group of men mugged him, severely beat him, and dumped him in an alley. He spent four days in a coma at the hospital until he died."

Reese was frozen in place. He looked pale.

"At the hospital, his mom didn't handle it well. She yelled at me and told me it was my fault he was dead because I sent him out so late at night. I was so upset that three days later, I miscarried."

"Fuck!" Reese spat. "That was—" He searched for words but ended up saying, "Fuck!"

"I missed the funeral because I was in the hospital."

Reese searched my eyes. "No wonder you don't wanna see anyone." He shook his head.

"It's not so much that I don't want to date. It's how...how everyone just expects me to move on with my life like those things haven't happened. I mean, they're all like, 'You should just find someone else.' And it's *so damn hard*." My voice broke over the last words, and the tears I was working to keep back finally overflowed.

Reese cupped my face with his hands and wiped away my tears with his thumbs. "Don't, baby. Take a deep breath and look up. Too beautiful a night to be sad. What happened, happened. Ain't nothing you can do about it. But you can help what you are now. And right now is what matters."

He wrapped me in his arms until my tears stopped running. It may have only been for a few minutes, but it meant everything.

He let go and walked backward. "Hold on for a sec. I gotta tell Steve something." He turned, I Intercepting Steve, who was loading a tray into their delivery truck. They exchanged words, and Reese jogged back.

The doors opened from the ballroom, and Charlie stepped out. I wiped my tears away and gathered myself.

"Damn it, Essie, sorry I left you alone."

"I'm not alone. This is my friend—"

"Hi. Reese Malone." Reese, who was taller, cut off my words and extended his hand to my brother.

Charlie shook Reese's hand. "Hi. Charlie Stevenson. I'm Essie's brother."

Reese's forehead wrinkled. "Essie?"

Charlie grinned and explained. "Essie has been

Sarah's nickname, forever. I don't even remember how she got it."

"Brianne started it when she was learning to spell. Sarah begins with the letter *s,* so she'd point to me and tried to spell my name. The *S* morphed into Essie," I explained to the men.

Reese nodded in understanding.

Charlie chuckled and nodded after the memory came back. "Oh, right. Hey, if you're okay out here, I'll head back."

"Yeah, go back. Have fun. I'll be in soon."

After Charlie went in and closed the door, Reese strolled up to me, extended his hand, and asked, "Care to dance?"

"Here?" I asked in surprise.

"Why not? The night is beautiful." He gestured to the stars. "You're beautiful. Great night to dance if you ask me."

His sweetness made me smile. I took his offered hand and wrapped my arm around his waist as he placed his palm on my back. We swayed to the muffled orchestral jazz coming from inside the ballroom.

His eyes roamed around my face with some emotion I couldn't identify, but it was intense. My heart fluttered. Awareness zinged through my entire body like that first night we met.

This was the most intimate contact I'd had with anyone since Jason. It was also the first time I'd brought myself to talk about what happened.

Why with him, of all people? Was it because our awkward first date had bonded us? Or maybe it was because, in some weird way that I couldn't put my finger on, he was familiar.

He twirled me around, cutting off my thoughts.

I giggled at his unexpected dancing prowess. After the song was over, he cupped my face again and placed a kiss on my forehead.

Reese pulled back and gazed into my eyes and said, "Sorry I left you at the café." Then he laid a small, tender kiss on my lips. We disengaged, and he walked backward while saying, "Gotta get back. Imma call, baby."

"Okay," was all I managed to say.

He grinned, turned, and walked around the side of the building where the service entrance was located.

I went back into the ballroom with a dreamy smile on my face. Charlie came up to me. "Everything okay out there?"

"Yeah. Everything went fine." Despite my bland reply, Charlie could tell that I was better than fine, based on his knowing smile that said he was in on my secret.

"Want to dance?" he asked, and towed me by the elbow to the dance floor before I responded. As we swayed from side to side, our sister came up to us in her beautiful wedding gown and asked, "Mind if I join in?"

We stretched an arm out towards her, and she joined. The three of us danced together. As we smiled at each other, an array of camera flashes went off around the room.

After the dance, I went back to sit at my table, and my phone vibrated in my purse. I pulled it out and read a text that came from an unknown number.

Unknown: Sweet. Thought you'd like to keep this.
There was a picture of me dancing with my siblings.
Sarah Stevenson: Who is this?
Unknown: Reese.
Sarah Stevenson: Ohhh.

I'd forgotten I'd deleted his number off my contact list the morning after he stood me up. I changed his name on my phone.

Reese Malone: Told you I'd call. Hope it wasn't too soon.
Sarah Stevenson: Not too soon. Thanks for the pic. :-)

Reese Malone: No probs. I gotta get back. Talk later.

Sarah Stevenson: K. Take care.

Reese Malone: You too, baby. ;-)

A white chef's jacket caught my attention as Reese made his way to the kitchen. We locked eyes, and he winked at me. My stomach flopped, and tingles ran through my body as I smiled back at him.

CHAPTER 13

*C*arol Lynne examined the picture Reese had taken of the three of us dancing at the wedding on my phone. We were sitting in the employee cafeteria, finishing our lunch.

"Who's the sex god?" Her eyes bugged out.

"If you mean the guy, that's my brother, Charlie. And eww. For real. Eww!"

"Nothing 'eww' about that." She started tapping the screen.

"Oh, I disagree, and what are you doing?"

"Sending this to myself. It's sweet. And his holiness of hotness will feed my dreams."

My expression must have been funny because she giggled when she handed it back.

I shook my head. "You have problems, woman."

"I speak the truth on behalf of all women not related to him. Your sisterly blinders make everything about your siblings seem gross."

She may have been right about that one. I could admit Charlie was handsome. But he was the type of man who knew it and used it to his advantage by charming women. That's all it took to get them to do what he wanted. *Gross.*

We stood up and said goodbye. Carol Lynne headed upstairs to her office while I filled up on more coffee.

"Sarah."

I glanced over my shoulder to find Gerald standing behind me. "Yeah?"

"You better come back to your desk. There's a problem."

Abandoning the coffee station, I hurried back to my desk. There was a note stuck on the desk that said HR had requested me downstairs.

"They brought your purse downstairs, so all you have to do is go," Gerald said.

My nerves went wild, and I nearly lost my lunch.

Moving woodenly, I made my way down to HR. When I walked into the room, a lady with salt and pepper black hair, wearing glasses that made her eyes look small, motioned for me to come over.

I sank down onto the seat.

She didn't even have to say it, but she did anyway. "Unfortunately, I have to inform you that you are no longer an employee of Sutter Communications."

"Why?" My voice sounded weird.

She looked down at her paper and read, "Not the right fit for the company."

Not the right fit? What kind of bullshit was that? I'd been working for four years for this company, and now I wasn't the right fit? Did they figure that out just now? Yeah right!

"Will you sign these papers? You will receive a severance check from us in two weeks." I signed the papers in what felt like a dreamy haze.

Once she checked the papers to be sure everything was in order, she said, "Here are your things. I'll ask that you leave the premises immediately."

I followed the security escort out of the building. I dragged myself to the subway station and made it back home, where I spent the rest of the afternoon crying on my couch.

CHAPTER 14

I sent out a mass text to Carol Lynne, Charlie, Dad, and Reese about what had happened earlier today. So it shouldn't have surprised me Dad texted that he and Charlie were coming over and were bringing dinner. They came straight from work because they were still in their suits.

We were having Chinese. I messaged him to bring extra since Reese and Carol Lynne had dropped in unexpectedly.

Carol Lynne, who was still in her work outfit of black slacks and an orange top, helped bring plates and spoons over to the gang. I went back to bring the drinks.

"So Reese. What do you do for a living?" my dad asked.

"I own a catering company. I deliver and set up the meals, and my business partner cooks."

Dad nodded, looking impressed. "Self-made. I like that."

"Thanks," he said. I was pretty sure that Reese was the type of guy who didn't give a damn who was impressed.

As I set the drinks on the table, Dad directed his questions to me. "So Sarah, what are you planning on doing?"

Before I could answer, Reese jumped in. "She could work for me. I'm sure Chris can find work for her at the commissary."

"There's also the pie offer. Now's the best time to start a business since you can now dedicate more time to it," Carol Lynne added, eating a plate full of lo mein with fried chicken on the side.

"What's the pie offer?" Charlie asked her. There were red splotches on her neck when he directed his attention at her. *Oy.*

"It's a business where Sarah makes pies and sells them through vendors."

"Sounds risky," my brother said, then stuffed a forkful of fried rice in his mouth.

"What's risky is not having a job. At least it's something. I don't see you offerin' up any bright ideas," my friend shot back, her southern drawl coming out.

Charlie's head jolted. He stopped chewing and stared at her.

My mouth dropped.

Carol Lynne was ballsy, but I thought she was going to be like the other women who he could wrap around his fingers, judging by how she'd reacted to his picture.

Reese was sitting on the stool by the breakfast bar. His lips curved into a smile. I swear, it never gets old. Those lips were so curvaceous, I wanted to lick them. It should be illegal for a man to be that hot. He made matters worse by winking at me. Fireworks went off in my stomach and my face heated.

Dad cleared his throat, causing my eyes to snap back to him. "Well, Carol Lynne. Great idea, and I appreciate you helping out that way, but she needs something that will generate income faster. Reese may be on the right track."

I frowned at Dad. "Don't discredit the pie offer so quickly, dad. I might be able to make a go of it. Besides, I don't know if I'm fired up to work for people anymore. It hasn't worked out in the past. Maybe this is the way to go." Thanks for the vote of confidence, Dad. He'd always regard me as a failure.

'*You haven't succeeded in the past,*' that shitty voice in the back of my head said. I concentrated on eating my meal. Luckily, the strands of my hair covered my burning ears.

"What name are you planning on using?" Dad asked, a little more gently.

I implored Carol Lynne with my eyes for an answer, because we hadn't finalized anything.

"How about Stevenson's Pie Mill?" Carol Lynne suggested.

Dad's face turned contemplative as he nodded.

Charlie spoke up. "We're gonna have to run that through the trademark database to make sure there aren't any names or patents attached to it."

My brother. Ever the lawyer.

Dad sighed. "Well, give it a try and see what happens."

His '*give it a try*' made heat crawl up my neck. I had to quit being this way. He just wanted to help.

My eyes met Reese's. He was studying me a little closer than I wanted. I flashed a closed-mouthed smile that probably showed how sad I was and looked at my food again.

"Run it through the website. I can have the ads printed right away," Carol Lynne told Charlie.

"Give me your number. I'll run back to the office and check, then I'll text you to go ahead," Charlie said to my friend.

She pulled out her phone, pulled up her contact list, and handed it to him. He programmed her number into his phone.

Reese smiled to himself and shook his head as he chewed his food.

After everyone eventually left, Reese brought the plates into the kitchen.

"Pie baking, huh? If you need help finding vendors, lemme know, because I may know some guys who could help."

"Thanks, that's sweet of you. I may need your help, but I'd like to try on my own first."

"What was up with you and your dad? Your back went up when he started talking. Or maybe I didn't know how committed you were to the pie business."

"I went to school for cooking. My fiancé wanted to open a restaurant. He was the aggressive go-getter type." I scraped food off the plates into the trash can. "After he died, and a few days later when I miscarried our daughter...I don't know. It was like my dreams, energy, and everything was buried with them."

"So if you can make a go of this pie business, it's like making things up to them?"

"Yeah. I guess." I turned on the water in the sink, soaped up the sponge, and began washing the dishes, then set them on the drying rack.

"Just sayin', babe, I'm here if you need my help with a job hookup. But if this is the thing you want, then try your best to make a go at it."

Reese brought over the glasses and placed them next to the dirty dishes. Then he stepped behind me, wrapped his arms around my waist, and kissed my neck.

After I was done, I dried my hands on the dish-towel, then grabbed his hand and led him to the couch. He flopped down, and I sat on his lap. Our lips joined. His hands ran along my body in a way that built a fire and comforted me at the same time. His sexy mouth made me forget my worries for the day as we made out.

CHAPTER 15

I spent the next day in a frenzy of baking, picking up ads and business cards from the printer store. Then, I ended up going to a department store and buying a few coolers that were stackable and attached to a dolly in the outdoors section.

My feet were killing me by the end of the day. But not having a job was so scary that I didn't have time to sit back and digest everything. I had to push forward.

The next morning I packed the cooler, a tote bag filled with signage, and set out to find a vendor.

By mid-afternoon, I was teary-eyed when I wheeled the cooler that contained the pies into *Bonicio's Delicatessen.* Patrons occupied every chair. Chatter competed with the shearing sounds of meat slicers and busy clerks shouting orders.

This was the seventh deli I'd approached with no luck. I waited in line until it was my turn to talk to the lady behind the counter. My mascara was runny from the heat and my hair had turned to frizz from the humidity. No wonder they weren't so keen to do business with me.

"Excuse me, I'm looking for the manager."

Benny, as his name tag showed, looked at me like I was wasting his time even before I spoke. Perspiration streaked down from the tips of his white hat-covered hair. It made its way down his face and settled along the collar of his wet white t-shirt. He wiped his gloved hands on his greased-covered apron and dragged his arm across his face to remove the moisture.

"Jimmy ain't here, and he never mentioned that he was expectin' somebody."

"Can't I talk to him, anyway?"

"Listen, lady, you can't walk in here sellin'. Now, if I can sell *you* a sandwich, great. If not, please leave the store." I thanked him, left my card, and walked outside of the deli.

At this rate, I may have to take Reese up on his job offer. The worry that had sat in the pit of my stomach all day only grew.

I maneuvered around people who were standing in line at a food truck. A few people from the back of the line abandoned their spot. Couldn't say I blamed them. I wouldn't want to wait in this heat either.

There was another deli around the corner I hadn't tried. When I got there and opened the door, the woman behind the counter gave me a dubious look as I came in. By now, that expression was far too familiar, and it made me want to do an about face and leave the store.

Swallowing a few times to clear out the dryness in my throat, I said, "Hi, I'm Sarah Stevenson from Stevenson Pie Mill. I have some pie samples I'd like for you to try."

She shook her head. "Not interested."

I didn't bother arguing with her because I'd been arguing all day to no avail. So I dislodged a business card from my clipboard and passed it to her. Then I rushed out of there before the tears I'd been holding back ran down my face.

I stood outside the shop, staring unseeing at the stream of traffic flowing up and down the street.

Why did I let Carol Lynne talk me into this? My entire family knew what a loser I was. Why couldn't I listen?

I wiped under my eyes.

Wheeling the cooler to the food truck I'd passed earlier, I joined the line for a late lunch.

The cook, who wore a black baseball cap with a logo design on the front, a matching t-shirt, and a white apron, shouted over the crowd at me. "Saw you walkin' up and down the block. You had any luck with that?"

The people who stood off to the side, eating their food, looked at me. It must have been so obvious to everyone that I was trying to make a sale. "No," I responded to him. My face heated at the attention. "No one is interested in selling mini pies."

"Mini pies? What, like tarts? No one wants to sell them? That's a quick sale. What flavor?"

"Apple," I answered. "Hey..can I get a dog and a Coke?" I asked.

"Sure, listen...I'd like to try the pie. You get me a slice while I get your order ready. Deal?"

"Yeah, sure." I paid for the food, then pulled a white square Styrofoam container out of my carrier and handed it over to him.

He folded open the lid, took one out, and took a bite. While he chewed it, his forehead wrinkled, which I didn't know how to interpret. "You baked this?"

"Ahh. Yeah?"

"You a baker or something?" he asked.

"A trained one, yes."

"A trained one...but not a working one," he clarified, and I nodded in confirmation and with a sheepish smile.

"What happened? Lost your job?"

"No...long story," I shrugged, trying my best to be dismissive, unwilling to share my story with a stranger.

"I'm Carlos...Tell you what...I'll give away your pies for free as a test run. Whaddya say to that?"

Damn. My hopes deflated like a popped balloon. "As much as I'd like to take you up on that offer, Carlos, I just lost my job, and I can't afford to not sell them."

I grabbed the clipboard, unclamped a business card, and handed it to him.

He read it and said, "Sarah Stevenson." His tone was contemplative, then he returned his calculating gaze to me.

"Right now, people don't know about your minis. Give them a chance to like it. They'll come back to pay for it. Look. I don't want to get your hopes up, but I'll text you later if this works. We'll talk more about working together. If not..." He pursed his lips and shrugged.

Was this really happening? I couldn't help feeling both disbelief and utter gratitude because this stranger had thrown me a lifeline. I didn't expect or plan any of it. I wanted to jump up and down and squeal with joy but didn't for fear that it would make me look unprofessional.

So I beamed at Carlos and said, "I'll be expecting your call, then."

After depositing the cooler at my apartment, I made an impromptu trip on the subway to the Spruce Ravine Cemetery in Queens. It didn't take long to locate Jason and Daphne's graves. The last time I'd visited was October of last year, on the fourth anniversary of their passing.

I approached the single gravestone, with Jason Brennan and Daphne Brennan engraved on the gray stone.

"You know, on the way here, I rehearsed what I was going to say. But none of it feels right," I said to the grave.

"For so long, I've been coming here and telling you how I've been doing. I lied. The truth is that I haven't been doing so great. But you probably knew that."

"I came here to offer an apology. Being alive and moving on didn't feel fair to you since I caused both of your passings. That feeling will never go away. But I can't honor your lives being how I was. The only thing left is to move forward and fight to make you proud. I will always love you. And everything I do from now on is in honor of you."

I placed a bouquet of rainbow roses in front of the grave, placed a kiss on my palm and touched the top of the gravestone.

Then I hurried out of the cemetery and to the subway because it was getting late. Being surrounded by gravestones was creepy at night.

After the 45-minute subway ride, my phone pinged with a message.

Carlos Gonzalez: Success, amiga!

Sarah Stevenson: Yay!!

Sarah Stevenson: I take it you're gonna need minis for tomorrow?

Carlos Gonzalez: Si. 100 by 5 am tomorrow.

Sarah Stevenson: Ok. I better get to work then.

Carlos Gonzalez: Si. Hasta mañana.

Sarah Stevenson: Thank you. Take care. Bye.

My body couldn't decide on panic or elation. So I settled for nervous excitement as I stopped at the grocery store to buy more baking supplies.

After I got home and changed into work clothes, I sent a mass text to the gang.

Sarah Stevenson: Found a vendor. Need to get some work done. They ordered 100 minis by tomorrow!

Ray Stevenson: Congratulations, sweetheart!

Carol Lynne Miller: Yay! Congrats!

Charlie Stevenson: Cool, Es. Way to go!

Reese Malone: Congrats, baby. Can I come over when I get off from work? I'll bring dinner.

Sarah Stevenson: Sure. Sounds great.

CHAPTER 16

*R*eese was standing at the door wearing a blue basketball jersey and shorts. He was holding two plastic bags. As he passed, he leaned down to kiss me, then set the bags on the breakfast bar and took in the mess of leftover dough and filling on the counter.

"Damn, baby. If I knew how to bake, I'd help. Looks like you could use it."

"I'm almost done. There's one more tray in the oven, and that should be it for tonight."

"So in the time you sent that message to now, you were able to complete a day's work to get ready for tomorrow. Not bad."

He would know since his business revolved around food.

"Yep. It's not like I have to run an entire kitchen. Just the dessert section, I guess."

"An entire kitchen would be a pain in the ass. Trust me."

I did since he'd been working in this industry for a while.

"Listen, babe. I'll dish this out, and you do what you were doing."

"Okay. The plates are in the cupboard. I'll start the cleanup."

We both set about our tasks, though he completed his before I finished mine.

When I glanced over my shoulder, he had already pulled out a few small, square Styrofoam containers filled with salad and set them aside. He was filling our plates with pasta Alfredo.

My stomach growled as the aroma of the food filled the air and reminded me that I hadn't had dinner. I hurried to place the extra pie filling in a plastic bowl and stored it in the fridge, then washed the dirty bowl and set it to dry.

He came over, stood behind me, placed one arm around my waist, and kissed the side of my neck. His rock-hard body pressed against mine and caused a low ache in my belly that had nothing to do with not having dinner. He opened the cupboard with his free hand, grabbed a few glasses, let me go, and went back to work.

"Ever heard of charcoal lemonade? I brought some."

I set the dough bowl on the rack to dry. "No, what is it?"

"It's regular lemonade that has charcoal in it. Tastes nice."

"Sounds interesting." And weird, but I didn't want to be rude and ungrateful.

The timer for the oven beeped, and I bent over to pull out the tray and set it down on the stove to cool.

When I turned, he was focused on my lower region. His eyes shot back up to mine.

He swallowed and looked at my lips, then back up to my eyes. "Yeah."

"If everything's ready, I guess we can eat."

His eyes went down again before turning away to the food. "Yeah, everything's ready. We just need forks."

I went to the drawer to grab a few, then walked over to the table and set them down. After we sat, Reese pulled the table closer, and we started on our salads.

"How was your day?" I asked.

"Total shit. We delivered the food to the wrong location because the customer changed the venue but didn't notify us. So we had to haul ass to the new place and were bitched at because we were late."

His phone rang. He read the screen, swiped so it stopped ringing, then returned it to his pocket.

The notification from the text message sounded right away. He rolled his eyes and pulled the phone out of his pocket again and read the screen, and muttered, "Fuck."

Then he threw out, "Be back," at me while walking towards the door to leave. His voice echoed in the hall. "None of your business. Oh, because you see me with someone else, that's only when you decide to call. Grow the fuck up."

There was a pause.

"That shit is getting old, and I'm tired. We're grown, at least I am, and it's time to move the fuck on."

A few seconds later, he walked back into the apartment, looking pissed.

I didn't know what to say but couldn't act like I hadn't heard what happened. Heck, even the neighbors probably heard.

"Your ex?" I said, trying to hedge whether this was a topic of conversation he was willing to broach.

"Yeah." He sighed. "Sorry you had to hear that. She's spoiled. She acts like a princess who throws tantrums every time she doesn't get her way."

He'd told me they were over. Why was she still calling? Or was it that he was done, but she wasn't? Damn.

I lost my appetite and put down my fork.

"She was bitchy back in high school. Her family is...connected. So she got it in her head that she could call shots and ordered people around, threatening them and shit like that. Most people didn't question her and did what she asked. Me too.

"Then she got bored and broke up with me. We were on and off in high school. But since I had to leave school, we drifted apart. Then when she heard I owned a delivery company, she tried to get back with me. But I didn't want any part of that anymore, because that life will only get you wacked. I kept away from her, but she's been back recently after she saw you in the coffee shop. She knows that I'm seeing someone else."

God. How terrible was that? He was trapped. His ex had sunk her claws in and didn't want to let go. It must be like living in jail.

We picked up our forks and ate our salads. "Is there something you can do? Like, get a restraining order?" I asked.

"Gia isn't the type to follow a restraining order. She's used to being in trouble with the law."

My brows knitted. "What do you mean?"

"Since she's connected, or at least her family is, she thinks she's above the law."

"How is that possible? Weren't those things a boys' club, no women allowed?" At least that's what it was like in all the movies and TV shows I watched.

"Doesn't mean that you can't pay someone off to do something."

None of this made sense. "She's got money like that to pull off a hit?"

He laughed and sat back down next to me. "Listen to you with the lingo. You watch mob movies?"

The nerves settled in my gut. Maybe I was blowing it out of proportion. "Nah. My father is in corporate law. I've heard things over the years."

"He dealt with a few jabronis?"

"More than a few in his time. I've heard some stories over the years. The point is, if you need help, we can always talk to my dad."

"Not that worried about her. Ain't jack shit she can do because her family connections don't got time to be dealing with her. She ain't no boss, and she'll never be. But enough about her. There's only so much of her I can take. Let's concentrate on us. You gotta tell me about mobster stories sometime."

The question tumbled out of my mouth before I could stop it. "You plan on sticking around?" I cringed. I was that girl who needed reassurances, and it made me feel stupid. But what did I have to feel silly about? This was an important question.

He answered by leaning in to kiss me. His lips were soft and his tongue tasted like coffee. That low hum returned in the pit of my stomach and goosebumps broke out on my skin when we parted. Then he gestured to the food telling me that I should continue eating.

I sipped on the charcoal iced tea. My eyes lit up. I could get used to this. I was expecting it to taste...I don't know. Grainy? But it was surprisingly lovely.

We kept the conversation light after that. He told me about his loud mother, doing impersonations that made me laugh.

After we were done with dinner, Reese did the dishes then laid on the couch and watched a basketball game while I packed everything away. As soon as I placed the last cup on the rack to dry, I bent down to the dishtowel hanging on the handle of the cupboard door and wasted no time drying my hands. I took a few calming breaths, turned, and met Reese's eyes. They followed me as my walk turned slow and erotic as I made my way closer to him.

He sat up on the couch and pointed the remote to the TV, turning it off.

I stripped off my tank top and dropped it on the floor. A slow sensual grin curved his lips and his eyes were filled with heat as his gaze moved down to my navy-blue lace bra. I unhooked the bra from the front clasp, letting my breasts free. Reese's hungry gaze made my nipples hard.

Opening the button on my shorts, I pulled down the zipper, letting it drop to the floor. His breathing sped up as his eyes dropped to the crotch of my matching panties.

I turned and stepped out of my shorts, giving him a view of the thong. Hooking my thumb in the side straps, I tugged it down, bending to let it fall to my feet and stepping out of it.

His intake of air was audible, and it put a naughty smile on my face. I turned to find him with his hand resting on his crotch. His steel-blue eyes were fiery as he took me in.

Then I went over to him and straddled his lap on the couch, grinding my crotch against it while covering his sexy lips with mine in a kiss.

Reese's tongue traced my lips before he plunged it

into my mouth and kissed me like he was trying to satiate his need. He let out a groan that vibrated in my throat. I broke off the kiss, stood up, and held out my hand. His hazy eyes were filled with lust and promise. He stood up and took my hand. We walked over to the light switch, and he flipped it off, darkening the apartment. Then he led me to my bedroom.

I went over to my bedside table, pulled the drawer, and took out a fresh box of condoms. My hands were shaking, which made opening the box difficult.

He let out a single huff and grabbed it from me, and ripped open the box in one pull, its contents spilling to the floor. He bent to pick up the blue line of packets and ripped one off, tossing it on the bed.

Reese pulled off his jersey and hooked a thumb in his underwear, dropping his shorts with them. His eyes never stopped their roving.

He shoved me on the bed, and I let out a squeal as I bounced on the mattress.

He climbed on me, kissing his way up my body towards my chest as I spread my legs wide. He veered off to my left breast, taking my nipple in his mouth. My back arched when his warm tongue fluttered. He moved to the other breast to give it an equal amount of attention.

I'd forgotten how wonderful this was.

Reese moved up to my mouth and kissed me while his hands glided down to the back of my legs and hiked them up while spreading me at the same time. He moved down my body, giving each nipple a lick. He continued down my body and licked my lower lips, making me moan. His warm tongue flicked my clit back and forth, making my back arch. His low groan made me vibrate.

Sweet Jesus, I couldn't withstand more of this. My body was electrified.

He reached for the condom, laid on his side, ripped open the wrapper, and rolled it on. "Too damn sweet. I need to be inside you before I lose control." Then his mouth covered my clit and fluttered.

I let out a desperate cry.

He crawled up my body.

I reached for his smooth cock and guided him to my entrance as he resettled himself on top of me, resting his arms by the side of my head. He thrusted to the hilt until he was deep inside, making him grunt.

The breath left my throat, and I jolted as the sting shot through my groin.

He stilled, "You okay, baby?"

I winced and gasped. "Yeah." I struggled to adjust to this new invasion. "It's been a long time," I assured him.

He stilled for a few more seconds, then slowly rotated his hips seductively. The sting eventually eased and was replaced by a dull, sensual ache that built as he moved. His hips revolved at a maddeningly slow pace. The restraint he exerted to ensure my comfort only deepened my feelings for him, yet the building need for him to move made me want to claw his back.

"Please," I cried out.

"Please what?"

"Please..." I repeated.

"Say it, Sarah," he said in a low growl. "Tell me what you want," he commanded.

"Move...I want you to move," I pleaded.

He kept up his maddeningly slow pace. Pleasure ratcheted up until it was aching and unbearable. I swear, if he didn't move...

"Please, fuck me," I begged.

Reese stopped moving, then thrust very hard and fast, letting go of his pent-up energy.

The sensation knocked the air out of my throat.

The headboard crashed against the wall in time with his movements.

My primal need was pushed to the brink until my body seized. An intense orgasm rocked me to the core.

I cried out.

His hard pounding kept up until his pace was frantic. Then he buried himself deep and let out a groan against my hair. He collapsed on top of me and rasped out, "Sweetness."

Reese rolled off and headed to the bathroom when I heard the toilet flush and the sink faucet turn on. I got off the bed to hunt for my clothes in the living room. After tugging on my underwear, I returned to the bedroom to turn on the window-mounted AC unit.

Reese walked out of the bathroom and got into bed.

I shimmied over to him, resting my head on his chest, and slung my leg over his. He slipped his hand inside my panties and cupped my left butt cheek. I nuzzled his neck and fell asleep.

CHAPTER 17

I delivered the pies and went shopping for more supplies. After depositing a crate of apples and a package of flour on the countertop, I left the apartment to have lunch at the bistro across the street with outdoor seating.

I'd passed many times and never eaten there. Never felt like it. But on a beautiful, bright day like today, I felt courageous.

After studying the menu and doing some serious soul-searching, I finally decided on the Pacific Northwest Hash, served with two poached eggs and a cup of coffee.

Sarah Stevenson: Hey butt-munch. Hope your game

went well.

Charlie Stevenson: You okay, Es?

Sigh. It blows that I couldn't initiate a normal conversation with my brother because he doubted my sanity. But it wasn't like anyone was to blame for that but me.

Sarah Stevenson: Arg!! Would be cool if you didn't act sus all the time. I mean, seriously!!... If I weren't, I wouldn't ask casual questions.

The phone rang.

Charlie didn't even wait for me to say *hello*. "For real, Es, you okay?"

My gut tightened. "Fine." My voice got a little louder to compete with the outdoor noise.

The server set my food on the cast iron table in front of me. I thanked her, and she left.

"Where are you right now?" my brother asked.

"The Western Sun bistro. The place across the street from my apartment. Just about to have brunch." I cut open my poached egg with a knife and fork and let it spill over the hash. Then I scooped it up and took a bite. I closed my eyes, savoring the deliciousness. I forgot how great poached eggs were.

"Just checking to see if you're okay. You usually don't make contact so I got worried."

My throat tightened, and I bit my lip as shame ran through my veins.

"Look. I wish I could take my behavior back, and I'm so sorry for going silent like I did. And, I have no clue on how to fix this except to move forward."

My brother said nothing to that, but I could tell that I'd struck a chord when he went silent.

He cleared his throat. "Dad and I were talking about how different you seemed, how you bounced back from being fired with that business. You seem a lot stronger."

"Thanks, bro. Oh, speaking of the other night, what the heck was up with you messing with Carol Lynne like that?"

He hesitated before he replied. "Look, Es, I just don't like her. There was something that bugged me. She's stuck up. Like she looked down at us. And I don't like how she named your business after her. It was too much for me."

"I know her; she's a decent person. She doesn't beat around the bush, and that's something you're not used to seeing. Plus, she didn't name the business after herself. It's a coincidence that her last name happens to be Miller."

"I don't think she's as forthright as you think. She has a motive."

Wow. He was way off base. "Oh, Charlie," I kept my tone light, "everyone has a motive. You should know that being a lawyer and all. Not all motives are bad ones. And that's the case with Carol Lynne. Plus, if it weren't for her, I wouldn't have anything to fall back on when I lost my job. She genuinely wants me to succeed. And she's never once asked me for money, and she has always been there for me."

I winced. *Damn.* I shouldn't have added the last part.

"Then we'll have to disagree on that point. I've got my eye on her to see that she doesn't cause you any trouble." He seemed unphased by my faux pas, to my relief.

"I appreciate your protectiveness, big brother, but I've got this."

He laughed, and I felt relieved. "Listen, I gotta get going. Is there anything else you need to talk about?"

"One more thing before you go. When are Bri and Troy coming back?"

"Wednesday. They'll be at the fundraiser on Saturday. That's if we have the fundraiser at all."

Fundraiser? The light dawned. *Oh my God.* Dad's annual fundraiser that he threw on his yacht.

"What's up with the fundraiser?" That I wasn't invited to.

"Not a big deal. One of the sponsors for the gift bags dropped out. So what if we only had five sponsors instead of six? But Dad lost his shit and is scrambling."

I wasn't really paying attention to what he said. The fact that they are having a party and hadn't invited me, when my siblings were going, hurt. Really hurt.

We said our goodbyes and hung up.

Without thinking about it, I texted my dad.

Sarah Stevenson: You're throwing a fundraiser, and everyone's invited, but not me? Is it because I didn't donate anything?

Ray Stevenson: Sorry, kid. You didn't seem interested in the past, so I stopped inviting you.

I didn't know whether to feel angry or sad. Both emotions ran through my body in equal measure. I forced my meal down past the knot in my throat and then rushed home to complete baking the order for tomorrow. I kneaded the dough with a little more force than necessary while doing it and wiped the tears away on my sleeve as I worked.

CHAPTER 18

*M*y crappy mood made me zoom through the baking process. I didn't even remember baking the four batches by the time dad's text came in.

Ray Stevenson: @ your door. Buzz me up.

My stomach churned. I wasn't in the best mood for company, and I didn't want to be rude to my father, which would probably be the case.

The footsteps of his Italian loafers echoed down the hall until they stopped outside my door. Then came a knock.

When I opened it, Dad stood there wearing blue

jeans, a mint green t-shirt that had a white tiger print on the front and a tight smile. I worked to not show my cringe as I stepped aside to let him by.

"Can't stay long because Connie and I are going to the movies, but I wanted to talk to you about the fundraiser and why you weren't invited." He got distracted by the tray on the stove. He picked up a tart and ate it. His face lit up.

"Kid. These are delicious." He ate another...then another.

I rubbed my forehead with my palm because he was eating product I had to sell.

He looked lost in thought for a minute before he asked, "Could you offer this at the fundraiser?"

"Offer it how? You want me to make these for the guests?"

"Yes. That would be nice." He looked at his watch. "Better get going. Connie's just leaving from work right about now. See you next Sunday," he said as he made his way out.

"Sure, Dad."

My father gave me a peck on my forehead and left.

That was quick and painless and a little odd. I returned to my kitchen to look at the damage Dad had done to the pie. There were only about seven left on a pan that fits ten. Sighing, I grabbed a few apples from the crate, washed them, and mounted one on the peeler.

I was about halfway done with that task when someone knocked on the door. As I walked to it, I asked, "Did you forget something, Dad?"

Reese stood there wearing his work uniform. I gave him a tired smile and let him pass.

"Won't be able to stay because I gotta head to the commissary to pick up an order for delivery. But I still wanted to say hi." He leaned down and gave me a quick peck on the lips. "Can I use your bathroom real quick?"

Ah, the real reason for the visit.

"Sure."

He put his phone down on the counter and went to use the bathroom.

I grabbed onto the crank of the apple peeler and turned it when his phone lit up. I bit my lip, picked it up, and looked at the screen.

Agt Smalls: No excuses. Get on it. We need to know where their money is coming from.

Another text came in from Gia Cantelli. A picture came in of a woman with long black hair. She was wearing red silk lingerie with a caption. *Just in case you forgot what I look like. Can't wait to see you.*

An explosion went off in my body.

He'd lied!

I threw the phone across the room. It bounced off the wall between the two windows. The toilet flushed, and the sound of the tap turned on. He opened the door and rushed out. His eyes were rounded.

"What happened?" His eyes bounced around the room.

"I've been played! After everything." Tears streamed down my face and my body trembled.

He walked over to the far wall to pick up the phone and read through the messages. Strain showed around his eyes, and his lips were tight. "You may as well sit down. I need to talk to you."

"Don't fill my ears with your bullshit."

"It's not fucking bullshit!! My fucking life is being messed with!" He put his hands on his forehead and massaged like he was trying to ease a headache.

I gritted my teeth and moved to sit down on the couch.

He sat on the other end.

"She's starting a faction. My job right now is to find out where she's getting the money to do so."

"Why do the Feds need you? Why can't they send investigators in?"

"They need evidence. If they send someone in, they might scare her, and she'll run off. They want to catch her first."

"And they need you for this? That doesn't even make sense, Reese."

"I'm being forced into it. I don't have a choice."

None of this made sense. Why would she be sending pictures to him?

"Do you have to be involved with her while you're carrying out this...investigation?"

"Yeah. Or at least pretend that I'm interested."

Oh, hell no! No way!

"Leave," I said through clenched teeth. His image danced behind my tears.

"Please understand," he countered.

"I understand that you're not a free man. I'm not willing to be the other woman while you are carrying out your...investigation."

"You are the only person who makes me happy anymore. You're the one that pulls me out of the pit I'm living in." Reese's voice had a ring of desperation that broke my heart. My tears spilled over.

I whispered. "Please, leave."

He shot up and stormed out of my apartment. The

door's slam caused the room to vibrate. I hugged the couch pillow and didn't move. Had I done the right thing? He was so sad, like he was reaching out to me, and I'd smacked his hands away.

But how could he not tell me that he was an informant?

That set off a fresh wave of tears.

I was so distracted that I forgot to finish my baking. I fell asleep sometime early the next morning.

CHAPTER 19

*M*y eyes flew open, and my body jolted into sitting. The display on the cable box read 9:15. Oh no! I'd missed Carlos' delivery! Snatching my phone off the table, I found two missed messages and a missed call from Carlos.

Carlos Gonzales: Not here. Everything Ok?
Carlos Gonzales: Opening soon, where are you?

It took a few minutes to pack the coolers with roughly 85 minis. My hands were shaking. I ran to the bathroom and put my hair up in a messy tail to hide that it wasn't brushed. I only rinsed with mouthwash and hoped that Carlos wouldn't mind.

I ran-walked up the block, weaving the cooler around people who were dressed in various work attire. They all gave me weird stairs while eyeing me head to toe. When Carlos spotted me, he glowered, and panic shot through my system. The same kind that I remembered having when I was asked into my ex-boss's office.

"Carlos, let me in around the back so I can load these up."

"Sorry. No can do." He shrugged like he was saying, 'Too bad.'

"Carlos. Please. I have your order here. Let me load these up."

"First, I don't do business with untrustworthy people. You have a job, and you didn't do it."

If he'd only listen. "Carlos. Please." My voice shook.

"I gave you a chance to prove yourself, and you didn't."

I winced as his words shot me in the heart.

"Please, I had a terrible night—"

"You think I care about your terrible nights? This world is filled with terrible nights, and we still have to get up and go to work the next morning."

My legs shook.

"Please, Carlos. Please let me work."

"Sorry. No."

I drew a step back from the van and stared at the pavement while tears rolled down my face. There was no point in arguing with him any further. It was like arguing with a brick wall. And what was worse was he was right. I'd blown my chance. I'd failed again. Failed Jason and Daphne. I kept failing.

I moped back to my apartment while trying to hold in my tears. After dropping the keys at the security door a few times while attempting to open it, I made it in. Hoisting the cooler up the stairs, I finally made it to my door. After getting in, I closed it and sunk down. Hugging my knees, I finally let loose and cried.

The buzz from my phone with an incoming message jogged me out of my stupor. My limbs felt like pins and needles as I made my way to the side table to answer it.

Ray Stevenson: Can you come over to the firm? Bring a few pies with you. I want to figure out how I could work them into the charity.
Sarah Stevenson: Sure, Dad. When?

Ray Stevenson: Will you be too busy this afternoon? Around 2?

Sarah Stevenson: No, that's fine.

What if I got a job out of this? My spirits lifted marginally. Something was better than what I had now. *Nothing.*

After a shower, I had a late breakfast of bagels and coffee. Then I put on a bit of makeup to look presentable and professional. In my case, that was bb cream, mascara, and tinted lip balm.

The yellow cab that I ordered pulled up in front of the building. After I made my way to the cab, the driver of the yellow cab got out. "Would you like me to put that in the trunk?" she asked in a cheerful voice and gestured to my wheelable suitcase. She had short black hair with long pieces that hung around her face and she wore a black, ribbed tank top and a black capri pants.

I wasn't sure if she could even lift my luggage because she was so petite.

"Um, is it okay if I leave it in the back? It has mini pies that I need to bring to my dad's office and I don't want them knocking around in the trunk." I explained before she got suspicious.

She nodded and opened the door. I hoisted the

luggage in the cab and she helped position it on the seat.

After she got into the front, I asked, "so what made you decide to be a cab driver? You usually don't see female cab drivers."

She said over her shoulder as we drove down the congested city street. "Tell me about it. Total sausage fest. But I like driving around, talking to folks. Actually, I've been thinking of switching to the night shift. More excitement from what I hear the guys at the garage say."

I scrunched my nose. "Dangerous excitement I bet. You'll have to deal with drunks."

"Suppose so. The vomit kit that I carry every day will be put to use. But the stories will be fun."

I shook my head. "Guess so." What an odd duck.

I made it to the building where Dad worked. His firm owned two floors of office space in Midtown Manhattan. After I paid the driver, I wrestled with the cooler to lift it out of the cab. The driver remained in his seat, waiting for me to leave.

Navigating my way around the sea of pedestrians, I made it through the glass door to a dubious-looking desk clerk.

"Whatever you're selling, we're not interested," he said with an unimpressed expression.

"I'm not selling anything. Ray Stevenson asked me to be here at two."

He looked down at his sheet; his gold-rimmed glasses slid down his nose. "Name," he demanded.

"Sarah Stevenson."

He peered at his list again and turned the page. "Sorry, not on here."

"I'll call up then," I said as I fished my phone out of my bag.

I found Dad's contact and hit the call button.

"Sarah, we're waiting for you," he said immediately.

"Dad, I'm downstairs. My name isn't on the list, and the doorman doesn't recognize me."

"What? Hold on." He hung up.

A minute later, the phone on the front desk rang, and the doorman answered. His expression changed while he spoke to Dad. Gone was his disinterested tone. It was replaced by a friendlier one.

My lips quirked to one side. Never failed. People acted one way towards rich people and another way towards people who they viewed were below them. I'd experienced both.

After he hung up the phone, he said, "You may go up."

Thanks, Gandalf. I nodded and flashed him a closed-mouth smile, then walked to the elevators.

I stepped onto Dad's floor with golden letters that said Stevenson Law on the front of the reception desk where a gorgeous redhead sat behind.

"Hello, I'm Sarah Stevenson. My Dad asked me to stop by."

Her moon-shaped face broke into a friendly smile. "Hi, nice to meet you. Mr. Stevenson is waiting for you in conference room two. It's down the hall and two doors on the right."

I already knew where it was since we came here all the time, growing up, but I didn't correct her.

"Thank you." I smiled and nodded and wheeled the cooler down the hall, and knocked on the door of CR 2.

"Come in," Dad's voice came from inside.

I took a few deep breaths to steady my nerves and pushed open the door.

CHAPTER 20

*D*ad sat at the head of the long table, while Charlie sat on the right side. An older, balding, gray-haired man with black-rimmed glasses in a light gray suit sat opposite my brother.

"Sarah, this is Allan Blair. He's our fundraising marketing rep at Sutter Communications."

Sutter. *Ugh.* Luckily he didn't recognize me, or else this would be way awkward for all of us.

We shook hands. "Pleased to meet you, Mr. Blair." I smiled at him.

His return smile was friendly enough. "Nice to meet you too Sarah, I've heard wonderful things about your new venture."

Wow, that was fast. Dad didn't waste time when it came to business. I blocked everything that had happened the day before from my mind and tried to concentrate on the man sitting across from me.

My father twisted to the sideboard behind him, opened the door and pulled a paper plate from a stack, and placed it on the table. "Could you please fill this plate with the minis?"

"Sure." I unlocked the cooler and piled them on the plate.

Dad said to Allen, "Taste these and tell me what you think. I thought that since we need one more item to fill the early-bird bag, we can add these in some kind of Styrofoam container."

Allen reached over and took a mini. Charlie and dad did the same right after.

"Can't be Styrofoam," Dad said while he chewed. "You need printed boxes with your logo design on them."

Their eyes lit up while they ate.

My heart fell at the mention of specially printed boxes. There went my savings.

"We can help with that since it's a branding issue. Can you have 300 pies baked for Saturday?" Allen addressed me.

"Yes, sir," I responded to him.

"You can use the kitchen on the yacht to prepare the pastries. We need them as fresh as possible," Dad said.

Allen put in, "You'll also need about 100 business cards printed up for the welcome bags. We'll need to know the address of your storefront."

I smiled and nodded at him, even though my nerves threw a party in my gut.

Shit! What do I do now? I don't have a storefront.

"Allen, we won't keep you. Thanks for doing me this favor in stopping by and for all your advice." Dad put an end to the meeting.

They stood and shook his hand. Then he made his way out.

I let out the breath that I was holding.

"Everything okay, kid?" Dad's face took on a concerned expression.

"I don't have a storefront. What am I going to do? I don't even use clever packaging. All I have is a product."

"How were you selling it before?" Dad asked.

My stomach fell. I was going to puke. I didn't want to tell my father that my partnership with Carlos had dissolved because I was irresponsible. Continually putting myself first and duty after. The precise reason why I was such a failure. "What's the matter?" Dad asked again.

"Nothing." I hoped that was convincing. My voice sounded startled. "The minis were sold in Styrofoam containers. Do I have to go into debt to buy special containers for this event?" I threw it out and hoped it distracted him.

Dad seemed satisfied by my answer, like he'd figured out what my problem was. He relaxed a bit. "No, don't worry about that. The reason I pushed that Styrofoam bit was because I wanted them to pay for the packaging."

My jaw dropped. This man was cunning. *Very* cunning. Charlie chuckled at my reaction. Probably because he wasn't surprised since he worked with Dad and saw this regularly. I rarely got to see him in *lawyer mode*.

"Don't worry. All you have to do is show up on the boat to bake the pies. We'll handle the packaging. Don't forget your business cards."

"I don't have a storefront though. We can't point the funders to a food truck." Not that there was a food truck. He looked off to the side, then met my eyes. "Lemme give that some thought."

"Not too long, because I'll need to print business cards."

Charlie spoke up. "How about online? Point them to a website where they can order them."

"I'll have to secure a name and set up a website by the weekend." And cancel my cable subscription to cover all of this. Maybe my phone too. God, that was terrible.

"Good idea, son," Dad said. Charlie sat up a little straighter. Dad continued, "Sarah. There you go. Website. Don't worry too much about marketing the site. You'll gain a few loyal customers through the fundraiser. Oh, please leave the pies you have in the cooler. We'll share them with the rest of the office."

In other words, he was taking the pies as payment. I couldn't fault him for that, because his help was paramount right now.

"See you Saturday, Es," my brother said and walked out of the room.

I smiled at Charlie and turned to my father. "Sure thing, Dad." I went over to the cupboard and took out three paper plates, and stacked the minis on them. Then I glanced over my shoulder. He was standing there, staring. "Yes, Dad?"

He gave me that same look he often had when I was little and lied about how much money I needed for lunch. The one that said that he was on to my bullshit and was waiting until I gave up the act.

"Thanks for everything," I said through emotion caught in my throat, giving the minis my full attention.

Dad walked over to me and gave me a comforting hug. That did it. My tears spilled over. He continued to hug me while rocking me back and forth.

When I got home, I researched domain names for the pie business. After seeing how much it cost to secure the website, I went over to my cable provider and canceled the cable. I could always reactivate it when money came in.

My heart hurt at that. The TV had been my constant companion for so long. I was losing my best friend.

The speed at which my life was changing was blinding. No job, no Reese. Nothing to look forward to, not even the television. Now I had to pay for a website that I couldn't afford as a front for my fledgling company.

How had this become my life? All I wanted to do was crawl in bed and not come out. But the last time I'd checked out, it had escalated my lousy luck and lost my pie income.

I paid for domain registration on a site that offered onboarding tools for professional-looking pages. For most of the night and into the morning, I set up my online business using photos Carol Lynne had sent of the minis. To my surprise, the website looked professional and classy. Thank god for templates and phone cameras.

CHAPTER 21

The restaurant on the boat was circular-shaped with windows that offered a 360-degree view of the water and harbor. The white drop ceiling had understated pot lights. Elegant teak posts were scattered throughout the space, and matching crown molding encircled the entire room. Blue-gray carpet covered the floor.

It hadn't changed from years ago, when Charlie, Brie, and I used to run around the tables playing tag. Our dad never let us play on the deck because he was nervous that we'd fall overboard.

Two crew members set up the ship's dining room, snapping crisp white tablecloths in the air and letting them settle on the tables. The other man set the table with items from a cart filled with plates, napkins, cutlery, and water goblets.

"Hey guys. I'm working in the kitchen."

They both acknowledged me with a smile and went back to their work.

I wheeled my rolling duffle bag to the back of the dining room, past the divider wall, and through a swing door to the kitchen. The room was deserted. The center island had a prep station and salad assembly. Fryers, stoves, ovens, and grills lined the back wall. Along the other corner of the room stood a vast stainless steel counter, an industrial mixer, and a dough sheeter.

Something felt off. Maybe it was because kitchens should have chefs running around, shouting orders at each other. Kitchens always had a busy vibe I loved.

The fryer was free of any trace of oil when I ran my finger inside. The massive refrigerator was empty and not even plugged in. It took some effort, but I wheeled it out, located the outlet, and plugged it in so that the dough could chill. Ingredients I requested stocked the stainless-steel storage shelves. Gathering and carrying them to the baking station, I emptied the baking supplies from my suitcase and began to work.

It took three hours and thirty minutes to make two hundred fifty minis. Something could be said for industrial equipment. A dough sheeter would have made my life a lot easier, but I'd have to wait until the money came in for that.

The swing doors opened, and the voices of men floated in. Keeping my back to them, I called out hello over my shoulder. They both acknowledged me with a "hey" and continued to wheel their cart to the prep area. The shelf under the counter was stacked with metal sheet trays. I loaded the minis on one of the sheets and brought them to the table in the dining room designated for the minis.

After unloading the pies, I twisted and bumped into someone, causing me to drop my tray.

"Woah," he called out and bent at the same time I did to get my tray. Our hat-clad heads bumped into each other.

Our stares clashed. When Reese's eyes met mine, his face dropped, and so did my heart. His eyes turned fierce, like the night we'd met.

Scrambling to my feet, I grabbed the metal tray out of his hand. "I take it you're catering this event." He stared at me, looking pissed.

"What. The. *Fuck*. Are you doing here?" he ground out. The dining room crew stopped to look at us.

I'd worked my butt off. This was my big night, and I

won't let him take it away from me. I lifted my chin and met his eyes.

"I'm working here tonight."

"Oh no, you're fucking not. Leave."

The nerve! The *fucking* nerve! "You don't have the right to tell me to leave, so do your job and mind your own damn business."

His brows hiked up before regaining composure.

Wait a minute. Why was he angry at me? He must have read the confusion on my face because his laugh was bitter. He shook his head and walked off.

I stared at his retreating back and tried to figure out what the hell had just happened. Then I remembered why I was there in the first place and went back into the kitchen for the rest of the minis.

We kept our distance from each other for the rest of the night while we set up. He gave me shitty looks from time to time but didn't speak to me at all.

"Sarah," Dad called out before spotting me.

I waved and said, "Over here, Dad." Everyone's attention, including Reese, focused on the man in the tux who came up to me.

"Honey, why aren't you dressed yet?"

"Dressed? For what?"

Dad looked at me like I was dense. "To sit at the table. We're about to start with the announcements.

Your friend Carol Lynne told me you'd be in the kitchen, while everyone else thinks you were a no-show."

My body felt heavy. I looked at my dad's black tie and said, "Dad, I'm back here because I have a job to do. That's why you asked me to be here. To work."

Dad looked stricken. "Sweetheart, I would never ask you to come to an event with family in attendance, and make you stay in the kitchen. I thought you'd join us outside after you were done back here. It's been so long since you attended a fundraiser. I wanted the rest of the family to see that you're doing so much better."

My eyes dropped to my feet, and I took a few deep breaths so I wouldn't cry.

He gave me a minute and placed his hands on both of my shoulders. Then he wrapped his arms around me in a hug.

"I won't be able to go out tonight. I'm all sweaty and look a fright from working." Couldn't we have this conversation somewhere else without everyone witnessing my humiliation?

"You take a minute, sweetheart, then come outside when you can. Everyone wants to see you." He let go of me and left the kitchen, leaving curious stares coming from the staff. I busied myself with packing my pans, rolling pin, and apple peeler into my suitcase. Then I walked to the double doors, paused to collect myself, and pushed through. My family sat at the front of the dining room. I pasted a smile on my face and greeted my family, who were already eating. The spot between Carol Lynne and Charlie was open, so I sat there. Her face looked relieved. I'm sure mine was flaming red, but I kept my chin up.

I folded my arms and kept them close to me, fearing that my armpits smelled from working in the kitchen all afternoon. My chef's cap was damp with sweat.

My sister was her usual beautiful and radiant self. I admired her colorful metallic, v-neck empire-dress. Her lush hair was down, and she wore long silver earrings that shimmered in the light. Her husband, Troy, sat next to her wearing a white suit. His vivid blue eyes were bright and his hand rested on the back of her chair.

"How was Bora Bora, you guys? Did you like the villa?"

Brianne beamed at me. "It was the best. We loved everything from the gorgeous view to the delicious food, and we even rented a private boat."

"Dude, you can operate a boat?" I said to Troy in surprise.

He chuckled. "Yeah, got my license before we went on the honeymoon as a surprise for Bri."

"Aww. That's sweet." I smiled at them. Troy

surprised me. Who knew he could be so considerate? I'd pegged him as a slime ball. Hmm, maybe I'd misjudged. All he needed was the love of a good woman.

A hand holding a plate of food appeared in front of me. I jolted and found Reese standing behind me with an unreadable expression. I pressed my lips together and nodded. He turned and walked back to the kitchen. My eyes were glued to his retreating back.

"What was that about?" My dad caught everything.

I shrugged, picked up my fork and knife, and started cutting into my steak. "My ex."

"Wait. What?" Bri asked.

I tried not to be offended by the shock in her tone.

"Oh, hell. That was the guy you were dancing with at the wedding," Charlie added.

"He was at my wedding?" Bri asked.

"Yes. He was your caterer," I answered her, paying very close attention to cutting the steak on my plate.

"Did you guys meet at my wedding?"

Why did this interest her?

"No, we met before your wedding." I put some food in my mouth and chewed, hoping it would discourage her from asking more questions.

"Wait. That company you suggested I call was your

boyfriend's company?" She laughed. "How did you two meet?"

Troy had the decency to jump in. "She said he was her ex. She may not want to talk about it, babe."

Seriously, my estimation of Troy was going up by the second. I tilted my head, smiled and said, "Thanks." Bri pouted. *Oh well.*

After dinner, Dad auctioned off a signed jersey, ball, shoes and a poster from a prominent basketball player from New York. There was also a luxury spa weekend at Balboa Bay in California. But the big-ticket item that caused a big bidding war was the new Benz.

I was worried that Carol Lynne would have been pissed or said something disparaging about corporate spending, but eyes were bouncing around the room, taking things in. Knowing her, she was taking notes. She froze my brother out, but he didn't let it bother him. He didn't even notice.

The photographers who were snapping pictures, made me want to hide under the table. The last thing I needed was them being published in the society section of the papers tomorrow. Perfect. Everyone looked like they belonged, while I was sweaty and wearing no makeup. I couldn't wait for this crappy evening to be over.

When the dinner was finally over, most of the

guests left the boat. Although a few stayed behind to chat with my dad and Charlie. I bid a hasty goodbye to my family, went back into the kitchen and fetched my suitcase.

The twinkling lights of the harbor were mesmerizing. I wheeled my luggage to the starboard side and leaned over the rail. I breathed in the briny air. It reminded me of seaside vacations to Martha's Vineyard. Dad had taken us there when we were kids for summer vacation. He nicknamed me *Sarah, Of The Sea,* because I always threw a tantrum when it was time to go home. I'd demanded that we sell our place on Madison and move there.

"Sarah," a deep voice called from behind me. Reese was walking towards me.

What now? There went what little peace I'd found. I turned back and looked out at the water.

"What are you doing out here?" He rested his arms on the rail next to me. His gaze was fixed on the harbor.

Finding absolution that only water can bring. I shrugged my shoulders. "Looking out at the water."

"Why are you alone out here?" he asked.

"What do you mean?" *And what is it to you?*

"Why are you here alone? Thought you would be the first one off the boat, with the speed at which you grabbed your stuff. I waited on the dock for you, and asked your family if they saw you, but no one did. So...I came back."

"I'm okay Reese, no need to waste your time. Steve is waiting for you." I wish he'd leave. I needed peace.

"I need to talk to you—"

Sigh. None of his words mattered when he was seeing his ex. Or whatever she was to him.

Hard lines etched his profile.

"*Sarah, of the sea!*" Dad's voice called out.

"Over by the rail," I shouted to my dad over the sound of the crashing waves.

"When no one saw you, I knew you were here." He stilled when he saw I wasn't alone.

I pulled my luggage towards him. "Don't worry, I won't put up a fight this time." He looked between the two of us.

"Dad, can you give me a ride home, please?"

"Sure, kid."

"Thanks."

I wheeled the suitcase down the gangplank and waited by dad's car. It took about five minutes for him to meet me there.

～

I made it home from the fundraiser. Someone knocked on the door while I was towel-drying my hair. I hurried to answer it.

The door was barely open when Reese barged through carrying a duffle bag and wearing a black tank and gray sweats. He dropped his bag, turned the locks on the door, and shoved me against the coat closet. He placed both hands on the side of my face and said in a low, intense voice, "Please listen."

My eyes flooded with tears, and my throat burned. "I can't. I can't be the other woman."

His voice was fierce when he said, "She's after me because she wants my business. She's doin' whatever she can to get at me. And I'm doin' whatever I can to avoid her. But know that I will always protect you. Always."

Reece swiped his thumbs under my eyes to clear away my tears and kissed my forehead. After I calmed, he kept on speaking. "You will never play second fiddle to anyone."

He continued, "You're it for me. When we danced, and you looked up at me with your sparkling eyes, I saw the universe reflected back. Our future, our kids, our life, and I want all of that with you. I told Smalls I was out. If they want to investigate, they'll have to do it themselves."

What?

"You can just walk away like that? And they let you?"

"I'm not an investigator. Just a delivery guy. Not gonna get involved in illegal shit to give them evidence. They have to get off their lazy asses and find another way to get their info. Send a cop in or something. Because that ain't my job."

I wrapped my arms around him, too overcome with emotion to verbally express it.

Reese's body tightened for a second. His eyes went from soft to intense. His lips captured mine, devouring me in a deep kiss. I returned his intensity.

He pushed his body into mine. I wrapped a leg around his waist. He lifted me, and I wrapped the other leg around him while continuing our kiss.

Reese ground his hips into me, sending sparks of pleasure through my sex.

I moaned into his mouth. He growled in return. I broke the kiss, my head falling back against the wall.

He carried me to my room and dropped me onto my bed. In a flurry, his tank went flying off to the side. He hooked his thumb in his underwear and yanked it down along with his sweats.

I only got my camisole off in the time he disrobed.

He pulled down my sleep shorts and panties so

quickly, the elastic snapped. After I was completely naked, he settled himself on top of me, his weight making me sink further into the mattress.

I wrapped my legs around his hips, my arms around his well-defined back. He drove deep with one thrust; his hips picked up speed. The headboard knocked against the wall. My back arched like a bow. The sensation intensified with such force that there was nothing I could do to stop my impending release.

My walls spasmed, and my body seized as the eruption of pleasure made me cry out. He increased his merciless pace. Reese's body jolted. He let out a wail as he planted himself deep inside of me. We stayed connected for a little while, catching our breath.

"Home," he whispered. I smiled and ran my fingers through his sweaty hair.

"Yeah," I whispered back. We righted ourselves on the bed. He got onto his back and settled me on his side. I tossed my leg over his body and rested my head and hand on his chest, and fell asleep.

CHAPTER 22

*R*eese sat on the couch the next morning while I prepared our breakfast. He only wore gray sweatpants so his muscled body was on display. He grabbed the remote off the coffee table, pointed it to the TV, and pressed the power a few times.

"Baby, your clicker needs new batteries."

"I had to cancel the cable because I couldn't afford to pay for that and all the fundraiser stuff," I admitted. My neck felt warm.

He studied me for a second. "Didn't know things were that bad. What happened to that vendor you were working with?"

The flush of humiliation crept up my neck to my

face. I really don't want to talk about it. "It...ahh...didn't work out." My voice got all pitchy. I tried for nonchalance but ended up making a face. "He reconsidered working with me."

"So you ain't worked since?" he asked.

I swallowed and confessed. "Last night was the first time in a couple of days." There was no point in hiding anything from him. Focusing on spreading cream cheese on our bagels, I tried to ignore the intense vibe coming from him.

"I could have helped you. Why didn't you come to me?"

I stopped what I was doing. "Why do you think? We broke up. I can't go to my ex and beg for a job. That's messed up."

His face flashed with disbelief before he smoothed it out.

Really? How bold do you have to be to demand things from your ex? Gia must have been something else.

Reaching for two mugs from the cupboard behind me, I filled them with freshly brewed coffee from the carafe, then added cream, sugar and gave them a stir. When I turned with the mugs in hand, Reese moved to the breakfast bar.

"If you needed help, you could've told me." His voice was so soft.

"I don't want you to feel you have to rescue me all the time. I've been a burden on my family for so long. I don't want to be a burden on you too."

"Baby, you'll never be a burden to me. Don't even think like that. I'm your man. I never stopped being your man, and I'll help with whatever you need."

My God, that's sweet. A warm smile spread across my face.

"You're staying over at my place since you don't have TV here. You can work and do whatever you want. After we eat, pack a suitcase with enough of your stuff to stay a while."

Is this man for real?

I hurried around the bar to kiss him. Which led to... other things. Oh well. We could reheat breakfast.

CHAPTER 23

That night, my jaw dropped as I walked into Reese's apartment. A hall led to an open concept living room with five massive windows along the far wall. The kitchen was to the far left and had massive cherry cabinets that stretched to the high ceiling. Floating shelves were mounted to the backsplash with pieces of eclectic vases and placed on each level. The countertops were black and held an assortment of kitchen appliances and a matching island with black stools.

Exposed, rustic beams ran along the ceiling. The walls were painted off-white, and in the living room, the beige couch sat across a wall where a massive television was mounted. The overall feeling of the apartment was airy.

I'd imagined him living in a place that was similar to mine. This was unexpected.

We sat on stools beside the island, eating leftovers that Reese had brought from work the night before. He was wearing black slacks and a light blue button-down shirt that was tucked in. His shapely legs bulged, and it caused a tingle in my nether regions. Tonight's dinner was an assortment of sandwiches and charcoal lemonade. Being with Reese was reawakening the adventurous foodie in me. It had been a while since I'd been curious about food...or anything for that matter.

"It must be like eating at a restaurant every day," I said, finishing the last bite of a ham sandwich.

"Yup, that's why I took this job in the first place. It came with perks. That's how Ma fed us when we were kids. You can save a shit ton on groceries."

I giggled. "Who knew shit could be so appetizing?"

A rich laugh burst from him that vibrated inside my core.

"This apartment is stunning. It seems... well put-together. Who decorated?"

"Ma. She has a knack for it even though her place looks dated. Told her that she could pro her decorating game and clean up."

Well. That made sense since he worked so much. Besides, it wouldn't be cool if traces of Gia were left behind.

"How long have you been living here?" I sipped on a glass of lemonade.

"'Bout four years."

Four years. My life fell apart four years ago while his was just beginning. Interesting how life worked.

"Where did you live before?"

"With Ma and Sammy. Sammy got a job working in construction, and he made decent cake, so he moved out. I stayed to help out Ma, but she met my stepdad, Bernard, and moved in. So I found this place through online searches. I wanted to stay in Brooklyn, and this place seemed like the right fit."

Reese must have busted his butt and pulled long hours to get this place. He was probably a workaholic, like Dad.

"What would you do if you had the time to go on vacation?"

"Get the hell out of New York," he chuckled.

He continued, "Go on a driving trip to see the mountains of Colorado or something. But work keeps me busy, so I never have the time. What about you?" He rested his palm on my leg, moving it under my skirt while eating with one hand.

"Um..." I lost concentration.

"What's the matter?" His voice was filled with false innocence as he ran his hand up and down my leg.

"Nothing." My voice came out breathy as goose-bumps broke out on my leg.

"You like this," he declared.

"Yes."

"I love touching you."

He'd said *love*. *Wow*. My heart did a happy dance.

Reese moved his hand and wrapped his fingers along the right side of my neck. He ran a finger down the spaghetti straps of my dress, continuing along with my breast, where he cupped and squeezed. His hand moved back up to just under my neck, all the while gazing intently into my eyes.

My breath caught in my throat. I wasn't used to a man being so bold with his touch. Especially when that man was as handsome as the one who stood before me.

"Beautiful," he said as he gently pulled my head halfway across the space between us, where he leaned in and kissed me. He stood up, not breaking our bond, and came to stand over me. He finally broke our kiss and held my gaze. His earnest, blue eyes searched mine. Grabbing my hand, he gently pulled me off the stool and led me down a hallway, past the TV wall to just outside of what I presumed was his bedroom door. He braced me against the wall and kissed me briefly, then turned me around so that I was facing the wall. He lifted both of my hands, placed them against the wall, and then pushed his body into mine, so I was pinned. He rubbed his cock along the crease of my butt. My dress crumpled with it.

Reese lowered his head against the left side of my neck and kissed me there while slipping a finger under the shoulder strap of my dress. He lowered the strap and moved to the other side, where he did the same. He peeled the fabric down, exposing my bare breast, then let my dress fall in a heap on the floor.

With one tug, my panties came down to join the floor pile. Reese sank to his knees and said, "Arch your back and hold on, baby." I did as he requested and immediately felt his tongue licking the seam of my lower lips, parting them, his tongue playing with my clit. I threw my head back and moaned, which caused him to moan in response. The vibration made my legs quiver.

I barely registered the sound of him frantically pulling at his tucked shirt because his tongue worked magic. The thunk told me that his pants buckle hit the floor. He dipped and turned so that his head faced the opposite direction, causing me to spread my legs wider. He continued to eat me like he was a starving man.

I let out a choked cry, a tremor starting from my center and radiating throughout my entire body, releasing the tension.

Reese moved from under me, stood up, grabbed my hand, and led me through the door to his bedroom. A large bed sat in the middle of the room with a giant taupe headboard. A large window was located on the far wall.

He walked backward until he fell on the bed. He laid back, displaying his impressive cock. His fingers gripped it, giving it a few strokes. He said, "I need your mouth."

I kneeled in front of him and wrapped my fingers around the base of his shaft. I ran my tongue along the length of him. I licked my lips to moisten them, then slowly slid him into my mouth as far back as he could go. His deep groan caused me to look up at him while I slid my mouth up and down, moving faster as I adjusted to his girth in my mouth. Watching him lose his composure turned me on. His hips bucked, shoving his cock further into my mouth.

He pulled my head off, grabbed under my arms, and lifted me so fast that I went flying onto the bed. He righted my body and settled himself on top. I wrapped my legs around his waist while he thrust in one swift motion. I cried out in a mixture of shock and pleasure.

"Hold on," he grunted out. I locked my arms around his back while he hammered fast into me. The speed and impact caused him to breathe quickly while grunting. It ratcheted up the intensity of my pleasure as I rapidly approached climax. An explosion shot from my loins, causing my limbs to go weak.

A few seconds later, his strokes moved deeper, his body coiling with more tension. He buried himself as deep as he could go and stilled. His warmth spilled inside. Reese collapsed on me, pressing me further into the mattress. He stayed for a few minutes before rolling off.

We took turns using the bathroom and settled into bed together. I nearly fell asleep when my man whispered, "Love you, baby."

"I love you too, Reese," I whispered. His arms tightened before relaxing again.

The last thing I remembered before drifting off was a sense of peace.

CHAPTER 24

My eyes opened to unfamiliar surroundings until memories of last evening flooded through my brain. The window blind was closed, but sharp white light poured through its spaces. I scanned my surroundings. My dress and underwear were folded and stacked on the backrest of Reese's office chair. My backpack and purse were on the floor beside them.

Reese wasn't in bed. My limbs and groin were sore, and there was a feeling of unease in the pit of my stomach. Waking up in another man's bedroom was a giant step. It was more of a dramatic change than having him over at my place.

I got out of bed, grabbed my toiletry bag and

some clothes, and rushed to the bathroom. I took a shower. The warm water did a lot to loosen my sore muscles. After getting out and brushing my teeth, I combed my hair into a ponytail. I slipped on a muted blue maxi summer dress with a white cherry blossom print.

The euphoria from the night before had subsided as I rushed into my routine. My stomach churned as the thought of no job filled my brain. I'd carved myself a refuge, and now there was nothing left. No apartment, no job, not even the calming distraction of TV. Nothing.

The mouthwatering smell of eggs, bacon, and coffee filled the air as I came out of the bathroom.

"Mornin', Twinkles." Reese glanced at me, then returned his attention to the counter.

Twinkles? That was a new one.

"You sleep okay?" he asked.

"Best sleep I've had in a while." I smiled at him while depositing myself on a stool.

"Me too. Could get used to you running around naked."

My face flamed.

Reese glanced up. His smile deepened as he arranged the bacon on our plates. He was being naughty and knew it.

Hating to bring her into the conversation, but

having to, I swallowed and asked, "Any more news about Gia?"

He looked at me again, but this time his eyes stayed on mine. "Told Agent Smalls that I only know what I know. I can't get closer to what they need, and that they have to get an investigator out to find out that information. I'm not gonna become an associate just to get them their info. To me, it felt like that's what they were askin'."

"I'm a delivery guy, not a field operative or whatever the hell they're called."

"True. Plus, I'm not sure whatever evidence you find would be admissible to fight a racketeering charge."

He looked at me for a second. "You know a lot about it, babe."

I shrugged. "Grew up around a law firm. I heard a lot."

"Thought you said your dad was a corporate lawyer."

"He is. They used corporations all the time to wash money. Dad has friends in the FBI. Sometimes he turns to them for help."

Reese raised his eyebrows as he poured coffee into dark blue cups. He took out a tin with the word "sugar" on the front and a carton of cream from the fridge.

I took a spoon on the counter, scooped the sugar in each cup, then poured the cream and stirred.

Reese leaned on the counter with his arms folded and studied me while I prepared our coffees. "Look at me, baby."

I stopped what I was doing and looked up at him.

"Nothing's gonna touch you. I made sure Gia was tied up with investigators. Too busy to mess with us before I came back. I'd never let anything hurt you. And she's after the money anyway. She doesn't care about me."

"I know." I continued stirring and put down the spoon.

"What is it then?"

I sighed. "It's everything. My life turned crazy, and I don't know which way is up or down. It feels like I'm being tossed around. And what's worse is that it feels like I'm losing everything I worked for. It's all happening so fast."

Reese walked around the island, stood before me, and cupped the side of my face. "You got me to help you work things out. You don't have to go through anything alone."

I shut my eyes and let his words move through me. The weight on my shoulders lifted. I took a deep breath and opened my eyes.

He leaned down and kissed me. "Let's eat. Then you can lay your problems out, and we'll figure it out."

He sat on the stool, and we had our eggs, bacon, and hash.

My phone rang in Reese's bedroom. He got up and went to his room, and returned with my handbag.

I dug through my bag to fish it out; it was a text notification from Dad.

Ray Stevenson: Can you come to the office?
Sarah Stevenson: Why? Did I do something wrong?
Ray Stevenson: No. Just business talk.
Sarah Stevenson: Ok. I'm at Reese's. In Brooklyn. I'll be there as fast as I can.

"Everything okay?" Reese asked as he chewed on his bacon.

"Dad wants me to go into his office. Says he wants to talk business."

"Okay. Finish your breakfast first. I'll drive you. You can come back here when you're done talking to him."

"While you're not here? Are you sure?"

"Sure, I'm sure, baby. Now tell me more about what's bugging you?"

I stared unseeing at my breakfast and inhaled, then admitted, "I lost the vendor."

His brows rose. "How?"

Heat warmed my cheeks, and I swallowed. "I overslept the night after we had the fight and missed delivering the pies. The next day, Carlos told me he didn't want to work with someone he couldn't depend on."

Reese ground down on his jaw while shame burned through me. Then he asked, "The day after we had the fight?"

"Yes."

"The day after we had the fight. You were upset, and when you finally fell asleep, you overslept." He said it like he was putting together a puzzle.

I chewed on my bacon and averted my eyes to my plate.

"Sorry, baby. I didn't know how fighting affects you."

"This isn't your fault. It's mine. I handle things badly. I always have. I put my own problems and heartache in front of my duty, and it has always failed me. It's just that I don't know how to control it. Once the heartache takes over, there's nothing I can do to pull myself out of it. I drown in it."

I drew a deep breath. "I want to learn to be stronger so I don't mess up everything."

He smiled at me. "Well. Start by finishing your breakfast."

I play-punched him in the arm, and he chuckled at his nonchalance.

"For real, baby, nobody can teach you to be strong. You have to wake up every day and do what you gotta do."

"Is that what you had to do? I mean, when your dad left."

"Yeah. We didn't have time for much else. Ma needed help paying the bills, so I took a job loading up trucks. Didn't have the time to get sad about it. It's shit that needs to get done. Pretty soon, I learned to operate more on duty and let my emotions take a backseat because, at the end of the day, it can't pay the bills."

That was admirable... and herculean.

"See? I want to learn to do that."

He said nothing for a second as he ate. Then he said, "What do you gotta do today?"

"Dad wants to see me."

"There. That's the shit you gotta get done today. The shit that's set in stone. Everything else in your life has to revolve around that."

I wrinkled my nose at him. "What do you have planned?"

"After I drop you off in the city, I gotta find Chris and see what places I gotta go to."

"So, like a meeting?"

"Yeah. I only gotta deliver to one place. It's a small office party, so I don't have to be there too long. But I'll be alone since Steve's out."

"When will you be home?"

His grin was huge and his expression said he was thinking naughty things. "Late afternoon, probably."

"Can I cook something?" I had to repay his kindness somehow. Maybe a home-cooked meal would be better than ones he had to bring home all the time.

"What do you plan on cooking?"

I shrugged. "Pasta and meat sauce? Honestly, it's been a while. I usually eat frozen meals."

"Why's that?"

"No reason to cook for myself. The only time I had a real meal was when I went over to Carol Lynn's."

"Guess that's changin' now since it'll be the two of us."

That tingle of happiness that had run through my body last night returned. The weight in my stomach had lifted.

He smiled and chugged his coffee. I did the same.

CHAPTER 25

J was about to get out of Reese's truck when he drew me in for a deep kiss that left me dizzy before he let me go with a smile. Ugh. That sly devil knew the effect he had on me and used it.

After I regained my senses, I said, "Thanks for the ride. Love you, see you later."

Reece's face was wiped clean with humor, and his expression stilled.

A pang of regret ran through my system. Had I revealed too much?

His eyes turned warm, and he searched my eyes. "Love you too, baby. Remember. All you gotta really think about is talking to your pops, and that's it. Take it one step at a time."

"Sure." No time like the present to practice. I got out of his truck and went inside.

A different guy was sitting behind the desk. "Hi, Sarah Stevenson here for Stevenson Law, 10th floor."

He checked his list and found my name, then he let me go to the elevators and one brought me up to the law firm. When the elevator doors opened, I walked to the redhead who sat behind the reception desk. Her nameplate read, Amberly. "Hi, I'm Sarah Stevenson, here to see Ray Stevenson."

"He's in his office. You can head on back," she said with a friendly smile.

I thanked her and walked to the back where Dad's corner office was. Charlie was in there, and he was just settling in his seat.

"Hi, Dad. Hey Charlie. You guys wanted to see me."

"Hey, kid. Sit down. We need to talk to you." A fissure of nerves hit me.

Dad started. "Your pies were a hit. So much so that I was thinking of ways to turn it into something. Now tell me. Whatever happened to the vendor you were working with? Are you still doing that?"

My stomach soured. "No, he decided he didn't

need me. So he terminated our agreement." No need to tell him how badly I'd screwed up, because I was already a screw-up in his eyes.

He nodded and looked at me but didn't say anything. After a beat, Dad said, "We've been talking about how the boat has been burning a hole in my pocket. The only thing that we use it for are the fundraisers, which don't really cover the cost of the yearly upkeep. So, we were thinking of a way to make it generate an income. Since we like your pie idea, we were thinking of setting up some kind of bistro or a café set up in that area."

My jaw dropped as my eyes bounced between the two of them. This can't be real. "But, all I do is make pies. A bistro is a long stretch from what I do."

"We can hire staff to take care of the rest. You don't have to do anything more than handle the pies."

Charlie spoke up. "I'll do research into the legalities and how we can go about setting up the business. After that, you can work there."

Finally, I had a real chance to make something out of myself. To make it up to the lost members of my family and make my life meaningful. Tears welled in my eyes.

Charlie leaned over and placed a palm on my back.

That was when I realized then that I was shaking. I leaned over and hugged my brother fiercely, in a way that I hadn't in a long time. Then I went around the desk and did the same with Dad. "Thank you," I whispered to him. I turned my attention to Charlie and said, "Thank you."

He nodded. His eyes were filled with emotion and his forehead creased.

I pulled away from Dad and returned to my seat.

Dad said, "By the way, Sarah. I dropped by your apartment last night to talk to you, but you weren't home."

Heat flamed my cheeks. "I was over at Reese's. He didn't like that I didn't have any TV, so he took me to his place." I tried to make that sound as non-sexual as I could.

"What do you mean, you don't have a TV?" Dad asked.

"I had to turn off my cable service to pay for the business cards and website since I don't have a job."

Both Dad and Charlie stared at me, a little stunned. That was the weird thing about rich people in the family. They didn't know what it was like not to be rich. They never had to take into consideration the financial implications for the poor in the family.

I shrugged, trying to affect nonchalance. "It's just

the way some things are. It's okay, I guess. I'll get it back. It's not really a big deal."

"Sarah. You live for the TV. For a while, it was the only thing you could look at. So don't give me it was no big deal."

"Dad, it's okay. It was just the TV."

"Not to you. It was your companion. Why didn't you tell me that things were this bad?"

My eyes fell on his desk. How could I go from so happy and grateful one moment to wanting to bolt out of there the next?

Dad prodded again. "Why, Sarah?"

"Because." I sighed. "How many times can I admit to being a loser? This family prides itself on winning its battles. And here I am, losing at every turn. I can't lose anymore!"

Why can't the earth open and swallow me up? This was more than I'd ever shared with any of them, and it felt awful.

Dad embraced me again. "Sorry for making you feel that way, kid. But if there's anything you need, you can always tell me."

Charlie came over and kissed my forehead. "Love you, Es."

"Love you too."

I left the office shortly after they told me to hang

tight while they got the research done. It still didn't solve my money issues, and I was a bit confused about what I was going to do in the meantime. Who knew how long it would take for all the legal work to come through. Then they'd have to remodel. More time added. I should probably find another job.

CHAPTER 26

a week later, I sat across from Reese's mom, Joanne, at a small kitchen table, having stew. She had blond hair that took on the texture of straw that fell to her shoulders. Her roots were darker. She looked like an older version of a rocker chick from the '80s that was animated and sometimes a little loud.

Reese sat next to me, and his stepdad, Bernard Krol, sat across from him. Bernard was a skinny, balding man with glasses and a goatee. He said little since Joanne was the talker of the two.

Their kitchen was small and cozy with little knick-knacks a la the '80s. A mixture of decorative copper cooking spoons and flowery dessert plates hung on the wall. They'd jam-packed it with stuff, and for some reason, it felt homey.

Joanne was staring at me a lot but smiled each time we made eye contact. I was still a little nervous. The only other parent I'd met was Jason's. His mom was super sweet until the last day I saw her, when she'd accused me of killing her son.

We were eating beef stew with mashed potatoes and biscuits for dinner. "Where did you grow up, Sarah?" she asked.

"The city. Dad has an apartment there."

She raised her brows, "What job does he do for a living?"

"He owns the Stevenson Law Firm in the city. He's a corporate lawyer."

She nodded, impressed.

"And what do you do?"

I sighed—tough one. "I'm a baker. My dad and brother are renovating a boat so that they can use it as a bistro. I'll be running it and baking pies. So right now, I'm in transition."

Bernard nodded, looking impressed. He said, "Must be some boat if you can fit a bistro in it."

My cheeks warmed as I chewed on a biscuit and nodded. "Dad uses it for corporate functions. But it's sitting at the dock, not doing anything. So they're turning it into a business that can earn revenue, aside from their main income from the law firm."

Both of his parents nodded.

Reese joined in, "She'll be running the online business until the bistro picks up."

That pit in my stomach opened. I had no idea if the few orders I'd gotten via the website would be enough to pay my bills while my father and brother set things up with the boat. I'd have to cancel my cell phone at this rate.

"What does your mom do?" Joanne asked.

Crap! I swallowed my bite of dinner roll and sipped on a glass of water. "My mother and I are estranged. I saw her at my sister's wedding a few months ago. And while I was helping my sister get dressed. Other than that, she hasn't been a part of my life, nor my brother's. But she's an out-of-work actress, so she does odd jobs."

Joanne shook her head. "Sorry to hear that, sweetheart. You have brothers and sisters?"

"One of each. Charlie is the oldest. He's a lawyer who works at our dad's firm. Brianne is my older sister. She's the middle child. She works at Northland Thread."

Joanne nodded. "Oh, right. Nice. When we're in the

city during Christmas, I like to go there and look at their holiday display. They go all out."

I agreed. "Yes, there's a planning committee for those windows. It's all kept a secret, and the stores try to outdo each other."

Her brows rose. "Really?"

"Yes. It's like a battle for window display. Somerset topped everyone last year when they not only decorated the windows but the whole front face of the building."

At dinner, I learned that Bernard was an adjunct professor who taught at the local university while Joanne was a homemaker. She'd had enough of the rat race, as she liked to call it.

Whenever our eyes met, Reese was already looking at me. It filled me with warmth because I wasn't accustomed to being admired before.

His phone screen lit with a notification of an incoming message. He looked at it, then his face fell.

"Trouble at work?" Joanne asked.

"Trouble with the ex," he answered. Joanne looked at me, but I glued my eyes to Reese.

"What's going on?" I asked him.

"She's threatening me again because I'm ignoring her."

"You said that we wouldn't hear from her since the Feds are investigating them."

Joanne's eyes widened at my words, and she looked over at Reese. "What Feds? What's going on? Is she in some kind of trouble?"

Reese's lips went tight, and his eyes went cold. Then he spoke to his mother. "She's in trouble with the Feds. They're investigating where she's getting money to run her operation."

"You told me before that she couldn't be a full-on mob boss because she's a woman and that I didn't have anything to worry about."

"No, you don't. I took the investigation as far as I could. Told Smalls I can't go in any further because I don't want her to think she can use my delivery business to launder money. My work is done with the investigation."

"Maybe that's why she's contacting you. That's what she's after," I said to him. "You're lucky you have commissary troubles because she can't find your base operation."

The three of them looked at me for a second and didn't say anything. It seemed like their cogs were turning.

Joanne asked, "Can you say something to the Feds about this? They can offer protection."

"I'm gonna have to contact Agent Smalls. He'll have to get involved because she shouldn't be in my face like this all the time."

"She's in your face? When?" I asked.

"A matter of speaking. I haven't seen her face to face since a few weeks ago. I told her I was too busy to talk and that I had to go to work."

My eyes opened wide. "She was in the apartment?"

"Not in. She came by. I didn't let her in."

"Why can't you tell her you're not interested in seeing her anymore? She's not getting the message that you don't want to see her." His stubborn pride was frustrating. Avoiding her only left the door open so that she could harass him. And me, by the looks of it.

"She knows that I'm not interested in her. It's like you said, she's interested in the business; that's why she keeps hanging on. These people go after known businesses to help them out with their operation."

My eyes dropped to the empty bowl. Dad could probably to do something.

I focused back on Reese. "I've offered before, but my dad might be able to help."

His brows came down. "Right, with his contacts?"

"He has friends in the bureau who may help."

"I don't want to get anyone else involved, Sarah.

It's bad enough that you know about it."

Joanne spoke up. "But if her father can help, wouldn't that be better?"

Bernard added, "Sounds like a good idea. Use your resources."

"You've been fighting this thing long enough. If there was a way to find your way out of it for sure, don't you think you owe it to your future to take the help?" Joanne said to Reese.

He stared down at his empty bowl and ground his jaw. Then he looked at me, his eyes moving around my face.

My breathing picked up speed, and I clenched my fists under the table.

He looked back at his mom and nodded.

I let out a breath and relaxed my hands.

"Excellent! Now that we have that settled, we can have dessert. I made Reese's favorite, apple pie. We can have it a la mode if you like." Joanne said.

My mouth dropped as I narrowed my eyes at Reese. He laughed like he was caught.

On our way home that night, the traffic lights moved across Reese's sculpted face.

I smiled as I asked, "What's your favorite dish?"

He glanced over, then back at the road with a small smile on his lips. "What Ma served tonight. Stew."

I arched a surprised brow in his direction. "I figured with all the fancy foods you eat, you preferred those meals."

He glanced over, this time with his brow wrinkled. The smile never left his face. "Naw. She used to cook that stuff for us when she had time. I always looked forward to it. Normal home-cooked meals are comforting. That stuff I deliver is more like finger foods. Snacks."

I studied the planes of his handsome face as a few things fell into place. "You like homey things. Home-cooked foods and comfort."

"Yeah," he smiled.

"My dad is like that," I said.

He glanced over at me again. "For real?"

"Yeah. He believes in family, memories, and he always talks to us over food."

"Looks like you take after your old man. You love to feed people."

My grin was huge. "I guess I do. It started out for different reasons. I was trying to have family meals in an attempt to keep my family together."

"How old were you when you did that?"

"Around eight or nine."

He glanced over again. "Pretty young to come up with that idea, babe. Where did you get it from?"

"I saw families on TV sharing meals around the table and noticed that we never did that. So I just made it so that we all ate at the same time. It didn't work, obviously."

His smile was tender. "Precious."

"Pardon?" My head tilted to the side.

"You, babe. You were precious to do something like that for your family."

Speaking of my family, that reminded me to do something. A smile spread across my face. I pulled out my phone from the front pocket of my bag and texted my dad.

Sarah Stevenson: Can Reese and I have dinner with you sometime soon?

Ray Stevenson: Sure, kiddo. How about tomorrow?

"Are you free tomorrow night for dinner with my dad?" I asked Reese.

"Yeah. I'm not working tomorrow night."

Sarah Stevenson: Tomorrow is good with us.

Ray Stevenson: See you then.

"Are you free to sleep over tonight?" I asked him. He grinned from ear to ear. "Sure."

CHAPTER 27

The following night Reese and I were sitting in the dining room of my father's apartment. We had penne alla vodka that he'd ordered at the restaurant downstairs.

While dad forked pasta, he asked, "So, kid, why do you guys really want to see me?"

My cringe was internal. He only expected me to visit when I had a problem. I'd been a crappy daughter.

"Well..." I didn't know how to start. "It's more like we need your advice. Reese was dating someone who got mixed up in trouble. They are being investigated, and they brought Reese in as an informant. The problem is that he supplied them with as much info as he could for them to investigate. While they're investigating, she's still making contact, and we don't know what to do."

Dad paused, eating, and his face darkened. With a tight jaw, he asked, "Are you still seeing this lady?"

Reese's brow furrowed. "No. She's after me because she wants my delivery business. She ain't interested in me."

Dad looked down at his meal for a minute before returning his eyes back to Reese. "Not interested. She's NOT interested in me." Dad's gray eyes turned to cold steel, and his mouth was dead serious. It was like he was a stranger, and it made me want to cut and run.

He continued. "What authorities are involved in this matter?"

"The Feds," Reese answered with hard eyes.

Dad said nothing, picked up his fork, and speared his penne.

I picked up my fork and moved the penne around my plate, no longer having an appetite.

He looked up again at Reese after a minute. "How long has this particular problem been going on?"

"Trouble started about two years ago when she got it into her head that she wanted to be the boss of her own family."

Dad fixed me with a stern expression when our

eyes met. I put down my fork. My arms hugged my stomach.

"You really jumped into a pot of hot water, kid. You just came to grips with your loss, now this.." He gestured over to Reese.

Reese stopped eating too. His jaw went hard. "We've already worked things out between us. It's not like I kept this from her."

I jumped in before Reese lost rein on his temper. "We're in love, Dad. I accept him. All of him. Even his troubles."

Dad let out a huge sigh, closed his eyes and massaged his wrinkled forehead. He opened them and said, "Tell me more about your business."

"It's a catering service. I drive the delivery truck. My partner runs our kitchens through a commissary. That's part of why we're safe. She needs a more permanent business."

Dad nodded. "She needs funding. I have a friend in racketeering investigations at the FBI. I'll contact her to see if there's anything that can be done," Dad said.

This was going so much worse than I'd expected. But I couldn't fault him for feeling the way he did. I was going to get an earful later tonight when he called and talked about why I shouldn't be with Reese. I was *so* not looking forward to that.

Dad spoke up; his previous mean face melted a little. "I have good news. The go-ahead for the bistro came through. So we'll be working on setting that up. You're gonna have to clear your schedule, Sarah, because I want you to be involved."

The dark haze I've been living under when it came to my career finally cleared. I have a chance to redeem myself. Not to mention, grab hold of something permanent. I grabbed my fork and resumed eating.

"When do you need me to be there, and for how long?"

"They're starting on Monday. They're setting up the front with the bistro cabinets, and they'll be rearranging the tables. Why, are you busy?"

"It's just that I need to get those orders for the minis sent out."

Reese joined in. "Are those places local? I could deliver them."

Dad nodded. "Not a bad idea. We could do deliveries."

Reese said, "Only for this run. I'd have to buy another truck and hire a guy to drive it because I'm already busy with my load as it is. But before doing that, we should wait and see how busy things get with online deliveries before deciding to take that step."

Dad's smile was small. "Makes sense. I like your business sense."

My shoulders felt lighter with a ton of weight lifted. Maybe I wouldn't get that phone call after all.

"Kid, since you're going to be on-site anyway, you can take the kitchen for a test run and bake from there."

My smile was a little subdued. I'd finally get to work in a proper kitchen. Finally.

CHAPTER 28

a few weeks later, the sound of the door closing as Reese went out for his morning jog made me turn over. My stomach rolled, and a wave of nausea ran up my throat. I got out of bed and dashed to Reese's bathroom, just in time as the contents of my stomach emptied in the toilet.

I rinsed the acid from my mouth and brushed my teeth while trying to deny what the tiny voice in my head whispered.

Dragging my feet back to the bedroom, I dressed in a daze, grabbed my bag, and left the apartment. According to my map on my phone, there was a pharmacy just around the corner. I went there and bought a pregnancy test, then made my way back to the apartment.

Some time later, I was staring at the toilet tank while sitting on the bathroom floor. The pee stick with a plus sign in the indicator window was in my hand when the door to the apartment opened.

This was crazy. I hadn't have any nausea except for this morning. Of course, I was tired, but that was due to physical work and stress. And I wasn't running to the bathroom every second. Wasn't that what pregnant women did?

Reese stood by the door, his hair wet, and perspiration ran along his neck. His black basketball shorts and white t-shirt clung to his fit body.

"What's the matter, baby?" He walked into the bathroom and knelt beside me. A second later, he said, "Knew it! I had a feeling last night while we were in bed that you're carryin' my kid. I knew it!" He raised his hands in victory. His antics sent relief through my system and made me giggle.

He sat down and pulled me onto his lap. I leaned against his damp body and rested my head on his shoulder.

"Baby, you okay with this?" he asked.

"Yes. I'm just surprised, that's all. Well...scared too."

He nodded with a blank expression on his face. "Me too, babe. Not like I had a good example of what a father was while I was growin' up."

"I didn't have a good example for a mom. Mine was a gold-digging actress who didn't want us. I don't even know where to go from here."

"We should get you to the doctor."

My heart dropped. "Doctors. Shit! I don't have any insurance now that I don't have work."

"So, I'll put you on mine."

"You can't put me on yours. We're not married."

He shrugged. "So, we'll get married."

I gaped at him. "Are you sure about this?"

He looked at me. His eyes bounced all over my face. "You love me?"

Wasn't that obvious? "Of course I do."

"Well, there's your answer. Cause I'm sure as hell in love with you. So, we'll do this. It's a little faster than either of us thought, but it would've happened, anyway."

He was right. But it wasn't just a little faster. It was a lot faster. Way faster than I was comfortable with. My life was moving at warp speed to catch up on the four years I'd missed out on.

"Come on." He pat my butt in a sign for me to get up. "We need to shower and get to work."

I got up with a little help from him. "Did you just say we?"

His smile was huge. "Yup."

"No mystery why I'm pregnant."

The smile never left his face. "Cause you can't keep your hands off me."

He was so right. I couldn't help myself when it came to him. I smiled and looked down at his chest.

Reese's fingers went under my chin and tilted my head up. "I'm the one who can't resist you. Your beautiful eyes and heart did me in. No other way to go."

My heart melted.

He lifted his t-shirt, then mine. Then we showered. And did other mind-blowing things.

The sound of drills and hammering filled the air while the work was being done in the ship's dining room echoed in the kitchen. I got lost in counting the finished minis instead of allowing this morning's news to take center stage. We'd decided not to tell the family until after I visited the doctor.

An unexpected saving grace in all this crazy was that the website had received a lot of orders. I still couldn't wrap my head around it. How the heck had they found out about me? That fundraiser was more beneficial than I initially expected. I wasn't rolling in it. But getting by was all I could ask for right now. That means I won't be kicked out of my apartment.

After the shower this morning, Reese said I should move in with him, so he could look after me. I had to admit, that was a relief. Dealing with pregnancy alone was frightening.

Packing the last of the minis into boxes and taping them shut, I stacked them on a dolly for the delivery guy to wheel into his truck.

"Hey Es. Checking on construction." I jumped a mile at my brother's voice.

He was here from the office, judging by his pressed white shirt and tan slacks. He grinned and gave me a hug, then rubbed the sides of my arm. "Easy, sis. Everything okay?"

I'm pregnant and can't tell you. Does that count?

"Yes. Locked in my head and concentrating on getting this stuff done." Well, that was true, so I shouldn't feel bad.

"Are you going back to the office, or are you done for the day after this?" I asked.

He looked a little taken aback by my question but tried to hide it.

Ugh. I should accept that my family would always regard me as someone disinterested in their lives.

I poured decaf coffee from the coffee pot that was sitting by my workstation, then placed a few minis from the tray and served them to my brother.

"How are things at work?" I asked, but he didn't answer because he had this funny look on his face while drinking his coffee.

"What's the matter?" I asked.

He sniffed at the drink. "This coffee smells and tastes weird. What is it?"

I chuckled. "It's decaf. I won't serve you poison. Quit acting weird."

"Since when do you drink decaf?"

Ah... "Since I've been on a health kick lately. I'm trying to clean up my act."

"Did you have to sacrifice the coffee, though?"

"Ahh, yeah. Pure body, pure mind." *I'm such a slug for lying to him.*

He rested the mug on the counter and popped a mini in his mouth. His eyes lit up for a second as he chewed, and I cheered inside.

"So, things have been going well for you and Reese?" Charlie asked with a full mouth.

Oh, thank God he'd changed the subject.

My grin beamed. "Yeah. Things are going really well."

He nodded. "You think he's the guy, then?"

"Yes. He's most definitely the guy. We've even been talking about getting married."

Charlie's eyes widened. "Whoa, Es, don't you think that's moving too fast?"

"Not at all. I don't see the point of waiting when we're gonna end up there, anyway."

"You've only known this guy for a little while. You two are definitely rushing."

My smile faded. "Waiting is more like wasting time. And in that time, your world can be taken away. You should do what matters. It's a regret that you'll never get over."

My brother's eyes shone with emotion, and he looked sheepish. "Sorry, Es. I'll butt out."

I shook my head. "I don't want you to butt out. Spent too long without my family involved in my life. It's just that...I wish you, Bri and Dad made some kind of attempt to understand why I made the choices I did."

"I get it, Es, and I'll talk to the rest of them about it."

Like he's the go-between? "Stop it, Charlie! Stop treating me like I'm not a part of this family. Stop having to be the go-between where you talk to Dad and Bri about the stuff I say. I want to say things to them myself. God, it's like you guys drew a straw and the loser is the one who has to talk to me."

The guilt on his face told me I wasn't far off in my guess and really hurt my feelings.

My God, he couldn't be for real.

I snatched my bag from the under-shelf, and stormed out of the kitchen, and stormed off the boat. As I walked off the causeway and towards the subway, something else penetrated my brain, even though I was upset with my family. A weird feeling like I was being followed took hold of my system. I glanced over my shoulder and at the traffic, but only a few black cars were driving down the road. Other than that, the street was deserted.

My phone rang, but I ignored it. These pregnancy hormones were doing a number on me.

CHAPTER 29

$\mathcal{T}$he following week, Reese held my hand while I lay in a hospital bed. The doctor moved a cold ultrasound probe on my stomach.

The little heart sounded healthy, but there was a faint echo that had me worried the baby had arrhythmia.

"Hmm, interesting." Dr. Brand said, and she moved the wand around vigorously until she found the source of the problem. "Ahh, here we go. Here's one heart-beat, and here's another."

Reese's fingers spasmed while we studied the screen while the doctor took measurements.

"After I'm done, I'll print out a picture of your babies that you can take home with you," she said.

Our eyes collided. Reese's jaw dropped open and his goggle eyes had the look of astonishment.

Reese spoke up, "Can you tell the sex yet?"

"Are you sure you want to know?"

We'd had this discussion before this appointment. We wanted to know the sex of the baby because it would be nice to figure out names.

"Yeah, we're sure," Reese said. I still couldn't talk, but I heard the printer go off.

"You're having a boy and a girl." Dr. Brand shot us a warm smile and handed me a black and white ultrasound photo strip.

She wiped the goop off my stomach with paper towels and threw them into the trash bin in the corner.

I examined the photo, trying to make out the peanut-shaped blobs.

Reese said, "They look like you."

A giggle burst out of me.

Resetting the equipment, she said, "I'd like to see you next month for another checkup. Feel free to use the bathroom." Gesturing with her chin at the door in the corner of the room, the doctor told us goodbye and left.

It was déjà vu when I entered my father's apartment that night because Charlie and Bri were sitting on the sofa. Charlie wore light blue jeans and a black t-shirt. He was more dressed down than I was used to seeing. Bri wore gray work slacks and a black babydoll top with puffy sleeves that fitted around her arm at the hem. Had she just come from work? With her, you couldn't tell because she always looked stunning.

I'd wanted to bring Reese tonight, but dad said, no, because he wanted to speak to us without our significant others' influence. Charlie didn't have a problem with this because he was *secretly* seeing Amberly Davidson, my brother-in-law's ex.

Why did he think it was a big secret? We all knew about it. It had to do with his fear of commitment, I'd bet.

If it wasn't for my pregnancy and thinking of all things I had to think about, this meeting would have bothered me. But right now, I didn't care. They can all gang up on me if they want.

My wave was half-hearted, and so was my "Hello." No one spoke as we waited for Dad to join us. When he walked into the living room, he was looking down at his phone. He glanced up at us, and his face fell. He put the phone in his pocket and gave us a short, "Dinner is waiting in the dining room."

We trudged into the dining room and sat in our spots. Dad sliced the lasagna and placed a square on his plate along with some of the Caesar salad. We did the same right after.

"They'll be done soon with the boat. There wasn't much that needed work since it was already a restaurant. We just needed to do some work to convert it to a bistro. Plus, Sarah, we are also giving you your own office."

Charlie's jaw closed, which made me angry because he had his own office in Dad's office. Apparently, I wasn't allowed to be treated the same way in this family. Or at least among my siblings. I stabbed lettuce with my fork.

"Thanks, Dad," I said, looking right at my father. My smile was more subdued than its usual spread.

"And," he continued, "we'll be having an opening party the night before."

We all gave half-hearted words of excitement.

His expression got severe. "Now, for why I invited you here. Sarah, you mentioned to your brother that you don't feel you're a part of the family."

The resentment must have been written all over my face. I glared at my brother but his expression didn't change as he held my stare.

"My question to you, Sarah, is why do you feel that way when we go out of our way to please you?"

I put down my fork and looked at my dad because I couldn't believe he'd just said that. "That right there is my problem! The three of you act like family. You talk to each other all the time. The only time you talk to me is when one of you draws the short straw."

Bri spoke up. "That's not fair, Es. We've tried to speak to you for years, and you shut everyone out. In that time, we all banded together. You can't expect to treat us coldly and expect to be welcomed back with open arms like nothing happened. When we tried speaking to you, we were afraid to say anything to make you cry or close off again. And it's been like that for years. The only reason you're talking to any of us is because you're with Reese now."

"What did I do that was so wrong? I was grieving over Jason and Daphne. Was that wrong of me? Was that selfish? I had a hand in killing both of them. Am I not supposed to feel something about it?"

They all shared looks of being stricken. I wanted to get up and walk out. But... I needed to stay and fight. To have this out once and for all.

"No one is saying that you shouldn't be upset," Charlie interjected. "But it was years, Es. Years of not treating us like family. And no one knew you blamed yourself for the death of the baby and Jason, because you shut down."

Shame seared my sternum. I wrapped my arms around my stomach to protect my babies.

Dad joined in. "We are glad that you found Reese. But we think you're moving too fast with him. Maybe if you two gave it some time before moving in—"

That's it! I shot up and pushed my chair back. It teetered and nearly fell over. Not staying for this. Before I left the table, I said, "I'm pregnant with twins. Reese asked me to move in with him so he can take care of me."

The silence was stunning.

I marched out of the dining room, past the living room, and was making my way to the door when someone's hand grabbed my shoulder and spun me around. Before I knew it, my face landed against dad's chest.

"Don't go," he whispered. His voice was hoarse.

My heart broke at his tender tone. More arms wrapped around me as my brother and sister joined in for a group hug which made me cry harder.

We stayed that way for a long while. I fought to regain composure.

After we broke apart, Dad said, "There's a celebration dinner that we need to finish in the dining room."

We walked back to the table, and Dad had his arms around my shoulder while we walked.

Bri asked, "When are you due?"

"April second of next year."

"Do you know what kinds you're having?" Charlie asked. I was tempted to say, human.

"Boy and girl."

Dad joined in. "Why don't we do a birth announcement with the family during the opening party?"

I shifted in my chair. "Ahh, Dad. Shouldn't the attention be on the bistro, not on me?"

"I get what you're saying, and that's sweet of you, but the family will be there, anyway. It saves on having to call everyone individually."

He had a point. It would be easier. "I guess if they're there. We can make a quick announcement."

"You're gonna need two cribs. Is Reese's apartment big enough for the four of you, or will you have to move?" Bri asked.

I couldn't help the smile on my face. "Reese's apartment is spectacular. And no, we won't have to move." I hesitated a little, then said, "You guys can come over to visit and see for yourselves. How about coming over for dinner?"

They smiled, and I read a bit of relief on their faces.

CHAPTER 30

*R*eese had just gotten the tray of pizza bite hors d'oeuvres ready and set it on the coffee table when someone knocked on the door. I hustled to the door, took a deep breath, then opened it. Carol Lynne wore a long black sporty dress and a white wrap that looked like someone's grandma had lovingly knitted it.

I greeted her and kissed her cheek. Her eyes narrowed when we pulled apart, then opened wide when she looked beyond to the apartment. "Holy crap, look at this place. It makes me feel like I can almost forgive you for keeping your pregnancy a secret from me."

That made me feel bad. I'd been a crappy friend.

"I'm so sorry. We just found out, then things went a little crazy during family dinner. This get-together is sort of like us mending fences."

"And I'm lumped into that category, huh?" Her expression turned wry.

"You should be included in family celebrations. Besides, we haven't seen each other in a while."

Her face softened when the doorbell rang. Reese went to open it, letting Dad and Bri through.

They both took turns giving me hugs and kisses and politely waved at Carol Lynne.

"Where's Troy?" I asked.

"He had to work late tonight," Bri answered a little too quickly.

"He's still at the office?" My nose wrinkled.

"No, he's working from home."

There was probably some game on TV he didn't want to miss. He wasn't really one to join in on family events, except for the fundraisers when the newspaper photographers cover the event. What did she see in him?

I nodded politely.

"You guys want the tour while we wait on Charlie?" Carol Lynne shuffled from foot to foot when I mentioned my brother's name. They followed me through the apartment while I showed them our bedroom and the nursery, which had unpacked bags with stuffed animals, diapers, and bottles. I'd lost my mind shopping at the baby store—so much fun. While we were on our tour, the doorbell rang, and the voice of Charlie sounded as Reese and my brother greeted each other.

Charlie was sitting on the couch with Dad in the living room. He wore a denim shirt with matching blue jeans and was chewing a pizza bite. His eyes lit up when he saw me but when his eyes slid to Carol Lynne, who followed behind me into the room, he chewed slower.

What was that about? Who knew. He was weird.

I went to sit next to my brother and wrapped my arms around him. This pleased our father, judging by the size of his grin.

"Dinner's ready, guys," Reese announced as he set a tray on the countertop. We'd laid the spread out on the island, intending to serve dinner buffet style. A tray of rigatoni antipasto, a side of freshly baked garlic bread cut into slices, and a Caesar salad sat on the island.

We stacked our plates full and sat around the apartment. All the men gathered around the television watching the baseball game. Playoffs or something, considering the way they were discussing stats and their general excitement.

"Are you going to move your furniture over here, or will you get rid of it?" Carol Lynne asked. She kept glancing over to the couch where the men sat. Did she want to watch the game?

"I think so. My stuff isn't this nice. But I'm going to bring all of my pictures on the walls." They both were looking around like they were trying to visualize my pictures.

"Are you going to paint the nursery?" Bri asked.

"Eventually. It'll have to wait until Reese gets time off."

Bri's smile was so genuine. "God, that's exciting. Two babies." Her expression turned serious. "Did you tell Mom?"

Dread snaked through my system. "Not yet. I should. It's just..." I shrugged.

She twisted her mouth as she forked at her rigatoni. "I understand what you're trying to say. But it would mean a lot to her to hear about it sooner than later."

I pursed my lips at 'mean a lot to her.' It said something that I don't know my own mother enough to know what things meant to her anymore. "I really don't know how Mom would feel about it since we haven't spoken since your wedding. She's never made an attempt to contact me." And as awful as it was, I didn't think she'd care because I was pregnant once before, and she'd showed little interest.

The rest of the night was super chill despite that weirdness. Reese was a good host, probably as a result of all the parties he'd catered.

Reese was in the kitchen cleaning while I sat on the couch. Taking my sister's advice, later that night, after my family went home, I decided to phone Mom. I scrolled through my contact list to find her number. After a deep breath to center myself, I tapped the call button.

She picked up after four rings. "Hey Es, everything okay?"

I rolled my eyes. If something was wrong, she'd be the last person I'd call. "Yes, Mom, everything's fine. I have some news I wanted to share."

"Oh? Good news or bad?"

"Great news."

"Okay, what is it?"

"Well, I'm pregnant," I said. My voice had a smile in it.

"What!?"

"I'm pregnant."

"Do you know who the father is?"

Ugh, here we go.

"Yes, Mom—"

"I mean, I expected this kind of news from Bri, but not from you."

"What do you mean?" All happiness dampened as my tone went flat.

She continued as if she didn't hear my question. "Well, I suppose it wouldn't be so bad now since Bri is married."

Her unenthusiasm was expected. My mother didn't like children because they interfered with your dreams. She treated us that way every time she left for an audition. But still. That dull, familiar ache returned in my chest because my mother couldn't care less. And I shouldn't feel that way because I knew how she was. But still.

CHAPTER 31

On the evening before the opening, we were in the dining room of the boat. I wore a goddess-style light blue gown with blingy shoulder straps. My hair was up in a loose textured bun, which gave it a soft, romantic look. I was overdressed, but didn't care, because I got to wear something nice for a change. It was nice being on this side of the fence.

Reese's brother Sam was cool, though they looked nothing alike. Sam was a tad shorter with brown hair and eyes. His hair was shaved at the sides and the top long, which he combed to the side. That, along with his goatee, made him look like a lumber-sexual. The twinkle in his eyes made him look like there was some kind of inside joke.

Sam's wife, Melissa, was a lovely blonde with delicate features. Her dress was long and pink and wrapped around the bodice. The rest of it was tulle. Kayla, their baby girl, wore a pink ruffle dress and lay sleeping in her mother's arms.

Reese's mom, Joanne's hair was crimped and clipped on one side. Her metallic wrap dress of silver, purple and pink with ruffles along one side made her look like she was attending a fancy party in the '80s. Bernard wore a brown '70s-style leisure suit with a cream satin shirt and a navy blue ascot.

Joanne shouted across the room at Bernard to speak rather than approaching him. And he always looked like he was trying to get away by feigning interest and walking off. Lots of times, he caught Dad's attention and gestured around at the boat. They were funny, even though I didn't know quite what to make of them.

Joanne pulled me close and asked, "Sweetheart, did you speak to your father about Reese's problem?"

"Yes. Dad said that he would look into it."

The relieved look on her face melted my heart. She must have been super stressed. I kissed her on the cheek.

She smiled and rubbed my arm. Then she looked around the room, searching for someone. When she located her son, she called out, "Sammy! Lemme see my grandchild."

Sam said, "Easy, Ma, you're gonna wake her." Reese focused on his sleeping niece. His face went soft.

I studied my man. He was more handsome than usual, in a black suit and tie with a crisp white shirt. The spikiness of his hair was tamed by gel and was side-swept.

"Thinking about what's in our future?" I asked, gesturing with a chin point in Kayla's direction. He looked at me. His face looked emotional, and his smile was warm. "Yeah," he whispered.

We wrapped our arms around one another and gazed into each other's eyes. I said, "Can't wait because I'll love every second."

He bent to place a tender kiss on my lips. When we separated, Bri held up her phone to show the photo she'd just snapped. She looked cool in a black romper with a fantastic gold necklace that looked like a chest plate. Her lips were super red, and her hair was up in a structured top bun.

"You two are so cute. Es, you're glowing," she said as she was looking down and fiddling with her phone. "There. Sent you a copy," she said. "Now, you'll have a few more photos to add to your album."

I hugged her and whispered my thanks in her ear. We held onto each other for a second when there was another flash. We turned to see Reese holding up his phone.

"Gotcha." He held up the phone for both of us to see.

"I'm surrounded by the paparazzi," I joked, which made the both of them chuckle.

Dad and Charlie walked over to join our group. "Reese, you still on for a game next Saturday?"

"Lookin' forward to it." He truly was. He'd tried to play it cool when he told me that my brother had invited him to play, but his excitement had seeped out. "Better check on them in the kitchen." He twisted and left—he'd been checking in on the catering staff throughout the evening to ensure they had everything under control.

It was difficult for him to leave work behind. It reminded me so much of Dad's work ethic. They share so many qualities that he fit in perfectly. It was like he was born to be here. Dad was still stilted with Reese because of the FBI stuff, but he'd made huge concessions after I'd shared my pregnancy news.

We lined up for the buffet once they readied the table. Reese surveyed the room, keeping track of what course everyone was on. After most people finished their desserts, he stood up. "I'd like to make an announcement." The room quieted down. "Sarah and I have been in love with each other for a while. She's moving in with me so that I can look after her because we're expecting twins next April."

There was a lot of cheering. Joanne's shout was distinct, "Oh my Gawd, a new grandchild." People came up to offer congratulations.

My sister wrapped me in a giant hug. She whispered in my ear, "Did you tell mom?"

My face fell. "Yes. She asked me if I knew who the father was." The reminder of that conversation dampened my good mood.

Bri winced. On a head tilt, she said,. "Honey, you know how Mom is. She can't help it. Forgive her for her shortcomings. Because of that, she can't be there for us in the way we need her."

Dad, who was standing behind Bri, said, "She's right. It took me a long time to accept that myself. She really can't give back because she doesn't know how."

I hugged Dad to placate him, but Mom should have known better, because she was a grown woman.

I had always been envious of others who were close to their mothers. Mom was closest to Bri due to their mutual love of fashion and the fact that my sister looked like a beautiful Amazonian doll. She was

proud of Charlie because he was financially success-
ful. And I was just... there. We had nothing in
common. I was interested in food, which she wasn't
because she was an actress. And more importantly, I
needed her when I lost Jason and Daphne, and she
wasn't there. I got to a place where I didn't feel the
need to talk to her anymore. When I dialed out years
ago, that was the one relationship where I didn't,
well... dial back in.

"Yes, Dad," was all I said. He shook Reese's hand
and said congratulations, then he asked us to reach out
to him if we needed anything and left.

After everyone was gone, and it was just the two of
us, Reese grabbed my hand and took me out by the
deck. The air was clean and salty. He pulled me into his
arms, shielding me from the wind. With our arms
wrapped around each other as we stared at the
bobbing lights on the pier for a while.

"You know I love you more than anything?"

My forehead wrinkled, "Ah, yes," I answered.

"And that I want to spend the rest of my life with
you, even if we weren't pregnant?"

Still confused, I answered, "Yes."

He reached into his pocket, got down on one knee,
and opened the velvet box. An emerald-cut diamond
surrounded by a halo of little diamonds on a gold band

glistened in the moonlight. My mouth dropped as I stared at it. My eyes welled up with tears.

"Marry me, baby."

"Yes," I croaked out. My hands trembled a little.

He took the ring out of the box and slipped it onto my finger. He lifted me up and kissed me. Our kiss turned fevered the longer we stayed connected. We hurried to disembark, went home, and celebrated in our special way.

CHAPTER 32

*R*eese was working at a charity gala downtown, so he wouldn't be back until tomorrow morning. I unpacked some boxes in my new apartment after getting home from work. As usual, the TV kept me company while I placed the framed photos of our family vacation against the wall. Reese had said he would hang them when he got home.

In one of them, Bri, Charlie, and I were building a sandcastle. At first, my brother had tried to play it cool, like he wasn't interested. Of course, then he told us that we didn't know what we were doing and took the lead in our architectural engineering effort.

While on those vacations, we'd stayed at a beach house in Martha's Vineyard. God, I'd loved those trips. I loved everything about that place. From the beach to the fourth of July light festival, it was so much fun. Best of all, we had Dad's undivided attention.

As I placed a framed picture to lean against the wall, an urgent knock sounded at the door. Reese had probably forgotten his keys, so I hurried. When I pulled it open, a short, voluptuous woman with long black hair, full lips, and a pretty face stood there, looking pissed.

She raked her eyes up and down my body and announced, "The bitch from the café?"

I swallowed. This woman was at my door demanding to know who I was? What in the ever-loving hell? I took in her narrowed eyes for a second. Did I have to call the police?

I modulated my voice to deescalate the situation. "Are you at the right place? Who are you looking for?"

"Reese," she stated matter-of-factly. "He's my man. But he hasn't been picking up, so I came by to see what was up."

The blood rushed out of my face, and I continued to stare stupidly at her because words failed me. This was Reese's ex.

"What's your name?" I asked, but I already knew.

"Gia," she answered while pulling out her phone to

snap a picture of me. She looked like she was sending it to someone.

Her eyes turned venomous. "Now, bitch, who are you, and why are you in my man's place?"

"I'm Reese's fiancée. I live here." I felt stunned, like a deer caught in headlights.

Her eyes flashed. "Bitch, I don't know who you think you are, but you don't live here. He ain't your man, he's mine, and *this* is *my* house." She was huffing and looked like she wanted to rip my hair out. She was about to attack at any second.

Gia was insane. My legs shook. I had to protect my babies. I slammed the door in her face and twisted all the locks.

She started kicking at the door, shouting, "Open up, bitch. Open the fucking door now!" She hammered her fists on the door.

I ran to my phone, and with shaky fingers, I dialed 911.

"Nine-one-one, what's your emergency?" said a female voice.

"My fiancée's ex-girlfriend is at the door. She's shouting and trying to open the door of my apartment. I'm pregnant and scared."

"Where is your residence?" the operator asked in a calm voice.

I gave her my old address then corrected my error. She said, "Okay, stay there. There's a unit on the way. Don't open the door and don't speak to her."

I followed her directions and stayed by the window while listening to Gia's histrionics while she was on the line. From time to time, the operator checked in on me.

The police car arrived outside the building after what felt like an eternity. "They're here," I told the dispatcher. I thanked her for staying on the line with me, and we hung up.

The banging stopped when the voices of two officers spoke up.

I went to the door and listened to the voices that echoed in the hall. Gia was crying and told them that I'd locked her outside, and I wouldn't let her in.

I reached for my purse from the hall closet and spilled its contents on the floor. From the pile, I took out my driver's license from my wallet. Thank goodness I'd changed the address because of my father's insistence.

The knock on the door was gentler compared to the banging earlier. "Who is it?" My voice shook. "The police, ma'am, please open up."

I unlocked the bolts and opened the door a crack to find a police officer standing on the other side.

"Mam, can you step outside so we can talk?" he said in a calm voice.

I tucked my keys and license in my pants pocket and stepped out. My legs felt like jelly. Gia gave me a shrewd smile as she side-eyed me for the briefest second while she spoke to the other officer.

"Step here to the side." I complied. "Please give me your name and tell me what's going on. Start from the beginning."

"My name is Sarah Stevenson. I recently moved in," I began, my voice shaky. "I was unpacking boxes inside when she banged on the door—"

"What time?" the officer asked. Jeez, I don't remember how long ago that was.

"The last time I glanced at the clock while I was unpacking, it was 7:30."

"Okay, continue."

"When she knocked, I opened the door. I thought my fiancé forgot his keys. But it was her. She said to me, 'Where's Reese, bitch?' I asked her who she was, and she told me her name. I told her I was Reese's fiancée. She said, 'I don't know who you think you are, but you are not his fiancée.' I got scared, so I slammed the door on her, locked it, and phoned nine-one-one."

The officer told me to wait right there while he spoke to his partner. Gia stood with her hands on her hip and shot me a victorious smirk while the officers talked.

Someone's footsteps echoed as they ran up the stairs.

"Sarah!" Reese called out. Everyone turned to look at him.

"Reese," Gia said, with relief in her voice. "There you are, sweetie. It took you long enough to get here. Tell these officers who I am, please, so we can continue with our lives."

Oh my God, this woman was out of her mind. I watched her, then Reese. What little strength remained disappeared. I wrapped my arms around my stomach and leaned against the wall. My legs gave out, I fell to the floor and cried.

"Baby!" Reese rushed over to me. He picked me up off the floor and wrapped his arms around me. "It'll be alright." He rubbed his hands up and down my back. I let out all the pent-up stress I felt and sobbed in Reese's arms.

The neighbors came out of their apartment to find out what happened. The police officer who had questioned me went around to talk to them. They all corroborated my version of the events and also said Gia didn't live there.

Reese reached for his phone in his back pocket,

flipped to the picture that he needed, and showed the officer all while holding me. Remembering I had proof of address, I showed the agent my driver's license. Because Gia had made false statements to the police officers, they took her away in handcuffs.

The officer said to Reese, "I recommend you file a restraining order. You folks have a good night." Safe to say, my night was shot to hell. I was going to be a nervous mess for the next couple of weeks. Reese and I went inside. The contents of my bag were on the ground beside the door. My wallet was splayed out on top of the pile. He asked me for my driver's license and put it back in the sleeve. Then he packed the bag while I stood there staring into space.

When he was done, he led me to the kitchen and made me sit on the stool while he made me a cup of decaf black tea with a little sugar and milk and watched me drink it. We washed up and went to bed. He lay on his back. I rested my head on his chest and threw my leg around his hip. He ran his hands up and down my arms, which calmed my frenzy in my stomach.

"I'm sorry, baby," he began. "I didn't think that she would do something like this."

"You've been ignoring her when she kept sending you messages. She'd show up eventually. You can't keep ignoring problems, Reese."

His hands stopped moving.

"She didn't do nothin' like that before. Never expected it," Reese said.

"You never ignored her in the past, huh?"

"In the past, no. I wasn't too nice to her while we were broken up, but I never really ignored her."

"It seems like she's a child throwing a hissy fit because she was never told no. Plus, shouldn't she be busy trying to dodge an investigation?"

He stilled and stared off in space like he was caught up in his thoughts. Then he kissed my forehead. "Don't know, baby. I'm going to have to see what's wrong with Smalls."

The look Gia had given me while she spoke to the officer had unsettled me. She had a look of triumph. What the hell did that mean? Was she that delusional, or could she pull one over on the police that easily? But she lied badly, so she would have been found out quickly enough. Maybe she got her way too often, and she didn't realize what it was like to mess up. Either way, she was messed up.

What in the hell had he seen in her? Well, maybe I shouldn't go down that road. Despite her craziness, she was pretty. She was voluptuous all over. I could see how someone could lose their mind for her. Maybe if you were pretty, you could get away with being crazy.

"What are you thinking about?" Damn, he'd asked the one question I wanted to avoid.

I can't handle hearing how much he'd loved her.

"What is it, baby?" Reese prompted again when I didn't answer.

"I was wondering what you saw in her in the first place since she's so damn crazy. But after meeting her, I could see why you kept going back. She's gorgeous," I admitted. My face heated.

He sighed. "We first hooked up when we were fifteen and in high school. To me, she was damn hot. Too much of a princess, but damn hot. She hung around because I had a job."

My body locked, and I swallowed. Throwing up a lot made me feel like I was ... well... disgusting. I never mentioned it to him because he would be obliged to reassure me. My pride could only handle so much. So hearing him talk about his hot ex was a little too much.

"I was a kid," he continued, "and stupid."

I sat up in bed. "You weren't a kid when she waltzed in and out of your life. That was a choice, Reese. At some point, you're going to have to put your foot down, because not confronting her means she can do whatever she wants, and you'll put up with it. But now, it means that I have to put up with it because she'll be in my life and my kids' life, and I don't want that. I'm not safe, and neither are my kids."

Sometime in the middle of the night, I got out of bed, walked into the living room, and sat on the couch. Bringing my knees up, I wrapped my arms around them and rested my chin on top. Some boxes were stacked and sitting in the corner, still unpacked.

For the first time, I doubted whether being with Reese was the best idea. Before this evening, Gia wasn't real. She was a phantom figure from his past. Not even after hearing the stories made it real. What happened this evening was a rude awakening. The truth about her and her insanity were dangerous.

Reese appeared in the doorway. He came out of the bedroom and sat down beside me on the sofa. He placed his hand on the back of my neck and massaged., then said, "I'll go down to the police station tomorrow and file a restraining order against her."

"Okay," I said in a small voice.

"I'll ask the police what else can be done to protect you too."

"I'll call my dad tomorrow and ask what can be done from a legal standpoint."

"Alright," he agreed. "Whatever it takes."

He took my hand and led me back to bed.

The next morning I woke up to an empty apartment because Reese had to leave early to load up the truck for a job.

Sarah Stevenson: Hey, Daddy.

Ray Stevenson: Hey, sweetheart. How are you doing on this fine morning?

Sarah Stevenson: Down in the dumps but still better than yesterday.

Ray Stevenson: What happened?

Sarah Stevenson: Bad stuff involving Reese's psycho ex. The police got involved.

A second went by before he responded.

Ray Stevenson: Where are you right now?

Sarah Stevenson: At Reese's

Ray Stevenson: Hang tight. I'll be right over.

Sarah Stevenson: Actually, Dad, can I come over to you? I need to get out of this place.

Ray Stevenson: Sure thing, sweetheart. I'm at home.

After explaining everything to my dad, he brought out a duvet from his guest room and a pillow and let me rest on his couch. My day was spent in front of the television. It was equivalent to crawling under a blanket and sucking my thumb, which I needed now.

Dad disappeared into his office, and even with the door closed, I heard him shouting at someone. I presumed it was at Reese because he shouted, "You better do whatever you can to protect her!" He stayed in his office to work but checked up on me intermittently.

Despite feeling comforted, my heart still hurt. I knew I was acting like a child, but I needed my father. He had always been the one who made things better. I don't know what I'd ever do without him.

When it was lunchtime, he ordered Italian food from his favorite restaurant. Dad had Bolognese, and I had mushroom risotto after convincing him I couldn't stand the smell the meat because of my morning sickness. We had tiramisu for dessert, and I could honestly say I hadn't had such delicious food for quite some time.

During the afternoon, there was a knock on the door that Dad went to answer. I was so engrossed in watching *Mary Poppins* that I didn't notice Reese had walked into the living room until he lifted my blanket and placed the bundle on the armchair next to the couch. Then he sat beside me. My throat tightened, and my heart picked up its pace.

He looked at me and held out his arms, indicating that he wanted me to climb onto his lap. I complied and wrapped one arm around the base of his neck.

"I left early this morning to go down to the police station to file a restraining order. After that, I went to the baby store with Dave and picked up a few things for the nursery. He helped me lift them up the stairs. I spent the rest of the time assembling the stuff and came here after."

What things did he buy? That had me curious, but I didn't ask right then because we had other more pressing matters to discuss.

He continued, "I was thinking about why you were upset all day."

"I got upset because you were talking about your ex-girlfriend being hot, and that was why you cut her so much slack. Plus, her crazy might get me and my kids hurt."

We heard a faint thump and a curse coming from dad's office. We both paused and looked in the direction of the sound. It was probably nothing, so I continued.

"With everything she put me through yesterday, all the fear, and the stress, and how she told the officers that she lived in the apartment. Just...everything. Last night when you were calling her your hot ex, I don't know. I just lost it. She can get away with anything."

He looked at me like I was crazy. "You don't think that you're beautiful?"

I swallowed the lump in my throat and shook my head. Especially not lately. Developing the sweats while I threw up didn't make me feel attractive. "Look, I'm not looking for reassurances. I don't need you to convince me of anything. I get it."

"You get what exactly?" His brows furrowed. "That I don't think that you're beautiful?"

I nodded. Heat crawled up my neck.

"Baby, last night, I was attempting to explain why I behaved stupidly. When I went back to her and tried to do the right thing and not be like my dad and just give up and leave. She knew that about me and took advantage.

"You're more than just beautiful. You are everything. Everything that I could ever want or need. I love you and my babies. I love you more than my own life, and I would give it up in an instant to protect you. You own my heart. Never question it."

Reese would give up his life to protect us. *Oh my god*. That was beautiful. My throat burned.

He cupped my face. "You understand that?"

I nodded as tears streamed down my face and

gathered by his fingers. He swiped his thumbs under my eyes, clearing them away. I twisted and grabbed a tissue from the box, sitting on the small side table beside the couch.

There was a knock on the door. My father rushed out of the office to answer it. Sounds of laughter came from the entrance, and dad walked into the living room with an older woman following. Her neat, shoulder-length blonde hair looked like she expertly wielded a blow dryer. There were laugh lines around her blue eyes. Her all-white outfit was summery and sophisticated.

She stopped in the living room to see me sitting on Reese's lap. "Oh Ray, I'm sorry, I thought I'd drop in. I didn't know you had company."

Dad made the introductions while I scrambled off Reese's lap to stand up. "Connie, this is my youngest daughter, Sarah. And this is her fiancé, Reese." We both took turns shaking Connie's hand. "Kid, you know Connie Paige. You met at your sister's wedding."

I went to hug her. "Hi, Connie. It's nice seeing you again. Actually, we were on our way out." I walked over to Dad and kissed him on the cheek. His troubled eyes bounced around my face. "Thanks, Dad. Thanks for everything." He enveloped me in one of his soul-soothing hugs.

"Love you, kid." His voice was raw with emotion.

"I love you too, Dad." He held me a few seconds longer before we broke apart. Reese shook Dad's hand and waved at Connie, then took my hand and took me home.

CHAPTER 33
REESE

*R*eese made his way to the boat as casually as he could so that he didn't tip off his ever-present audience, which wasn't too hard since he was dog-tired from stress and lack of sleep.

The question that bounced around in his brain was how to protect Sarah while neutralizing Gia? The FBI did fuck-all to help. They didn't want to make moves until she did something illegal, like take his business. And he doubted Ray had a contact in the organization, because no one had reached out to him.

He was in her line of sight because she was after his business. His only saving grace was that she was the new kid on the block, and the other guys don't like territory squatters. It may be a long shot, but he might be able to turn them against Gia.

Reese walked straight to Sarah's office and found her sleeping on her blue velvet couch, covered by a cream-colored blanket. Her head rested on a pillow, and she looked like an angel. His angel. The one he had to protect.

He took a much-needed seat by her desk and stared off into space, his mind racing. They needed to get married, asap. He wanted her to be his wife. Should anything happen to him, she would inherit his business. She could sell her part of it so that she and his kids could live comfortably for the rest of their lives. They'd be married if he survived. That was all he'd ever wanted, anyway.

Sarah opened her eyes and gasped a little when she saw him. He smiled warmly at her. "You had a good nap, baby?"

She nodded groggily. "I thought you were sending Steve to pick me up." She sat up and looked around, confused.

"It's not time for you to be picked up. It's still morning. I just wanted to see you, that's all."

She waved goofily at him and said, "Hi."

That made him chuckle. That was his Sarah, always making him laugh even though she never intended to.

"How about you and me leave for Atlantic City this weekend?" he said suddenly.

"Like on a trip?" She mulled it over for a second. Her eyes studied the dark circles under his.

"Sounds nice. I'll need to brief Maggie on a few things before we leave."

"Okay, no problem. I'll be back to pick you up tonight. We'll go to the apartment to pack a few things. I'll also reserve a room." The honeymoon suite. But he didn't say that to her.

"Sure." Her voice cracked with excitement. Her gray eyes were alight. Those eyes had made him fall in love with her. So pure, you could see deep into her soul. The other night when she'd told him so matter-of-factly that she didn't think she was beautiful, it had broken his heart. She was more than beautiful.

It made him feel shitty for talking about Gia the way he had and hurting his girl's feelings. Gia couldn't hold a candle to his Sarah. No one could.

CHAPTER 34

They were almost at their destination in New Jersey. Throughout the drive, Sarah gave him curious glances, like she suspected something was off.

Reese glanced at his girl. "What's up, babe?"

She shrugged and smiled back. "Nothing. This is different. You rarely take time off work. Don't get me wrong," she hurried to smooth over, "I love it, but this is... different."

"I get you. I never take time off. Didn't have a reason. But now, things are changing, so I will too. Not a lot of time off, but some now and again ain't bad."

"That sounds like something my dad would say."

She'd said something similar in the past, but he

wanted to keep her talking. He quirked up a brow at her because he knew that she loved that expression. "Really?" he prompted. This was a safer topic since he didn't want to talk about the boat. It was a future that he wasn't sure he'd be a part of.

"He's a work-a-holic. But, he loved us and would schedule family vacations every year. We'd go to Martha's Vineyard and had a blast. We stopped going when Charlie went off to college because Dad didn't want him to feel left out."

Did she have good memories of Gabrielle? She only spoke about her dad and sibs. "Did your mom ever go with you guys?"

Sarah's nose scrunched for a second, which he thought was adorable. "No, he didn't invite her along. He was fed up with the entire situation by the time their divorce was final. The sad part was that she would always bring her boyfriend actors when they were forced to be in the same room together. Charlie, Bri, and I differ on this because they think Dad is still in love with Mom, but I don't."

"Why do you view the situation differently than your sibs?" Reese asked.

"Wishful thinking, ya know? They wanted to think that there's a chance that Mom and Dad could get together. But I spent so much time with Mom that honestly, I didn't understand what he saw in her in the first place. And I know that it's a shitty thing to say because she's my mom. But when I lost my first baby and she wasn't there for me, it pulled the wool from my eyes about who she was. She doesn't care."

He searched around for something to say to console her because that sounded damn sad. "Don't worry about it, babe. We can share my mom. She doesn't have a daughter, so she'll be down with that. That's if you don't mind having a loud mom."

Her laughter made her eyes twinkle and his stomach flutter.

A massive king bed was in the middle of the suite. On it were rose petals sprinkled in a heart shape that greeted them when they opened the door.

Inside the heart sat a white platter with strawberries dipped in a selection of chocolates.

Further up the bed were towels folded to look like two swans kissing. Their tails looked like fans. On the side table next to the bed sat an ice bucket with a bottle of champagne inside. Beyond the bed was a wall-sized window with an ocean view.

Sarah took in the romantic scene. She turned, giving Reese a puzzled expression.

"Did they give us this room by mistake... because this is a—"

"No mistake." Reese walked to her, his throat tightened, and palms sweaty.

"Baby... Sarah, will you marry me here this weekend?"

She stood there gaping at him. "I...I...you...you want to do this now, instead of in front of our families?"

Reese swallowed. "I wanted to be married to you that first night we danced together. We can get married now and have a reception with our families later."

"Why can't we wait until our families can attend and do it all at once?"

"Because that will be after the babies are born, and I want to be married before then." Well, that was partially true. He wanted to get married as soon as possible, but it wasn't precisely for those reasons. The worst of it was that he couldn't tell her why because it would put her in danger.

A shadow crossed Sarah's face. "I don't want to get married because you feel forced, Reese."

"Trust me. No one is forcing me to marry you. I would have married you that night we danced together at your sister's wedding. You are what I want most in the world, and we're engaged. I know we haven't talked about it because of everything going down with the babies and boat. But if we make it official now, it's one less thing to worry about. We could have a reception sometime down the road." He hoped that his speech was convincing, because they needed to get married.

Sarah's face softened. "Well, less stress is a good thing, and this room is so beautiful. It would be a shame to see it go to waste."

Reese beamed and took his girl's hand. "Come on, let me show you around."

He led her to the bathroom, reached in to switch on the lights, and let her walk in. Her eyes went wide as she took in the large Jacuzzi tub with more rose petals sprinkled inside. The surrounding shelf had unlit tea candles. Next to the tub stood a sizable glass-walled shower with a rainfall showerhead. On the opposite wall stood a beautiful double sink vanity and a massive mirror. Between the sinks sat a bamboo tray filled with soap, shampoo, and conditioner bottles, and a stack of folded white towels.

Even though she'd grown up in a wealthy family, her father had never flaunted his wealth. He had a very humble attitude since their wealth was genera-tional, so there was time to acclimate. Owning luxurious items and staying in posh hotels wasn't something they did. Granted, he drove a BMW and owned a boat, but you couldn't tell that he was well off beyond that.

Reese, on the other hand, owned a fancy apartment in a wealthy part of Brooklyn. He decorated his home nicely and lived comfortably. His business was thriving but he came from humble beginnings. Sometimes he liked to show off his good fortune, and indeed, this was such a time.

Sarah looked at him with a big goofy grin. She raised their entwined hands and kissed his. "I love this." She hugged him. "Thank you so very much."

He smiled. "Love you," he said, then kissed the top of her head. "We can put the tub to use later. And the champagne outside is non-alcoholic, so you can drink to your heart's delight."

"You are so thoughtful. Another reason I'm glad that I'm marrying you." Her face fell in an instant. "I don't have a dress. I didn't pack anything white that I can use."

"We can pick one out at the boutique downstairs before we head out to the Clarke County office."

"Okay," she warmed further at the thought. "This should be fun."

"I filled out the marriage license document a few

days ago, so the process will be quicker. We don't have to wait in long lines."

Sarah glanced at his lips, then his eyes. It brought a smile to his lips, and he pulled her close. They kissed deeply, which soon ignited into a passion. He broke away from her, panting. "Baby, we gotta wait until after the ceremony, so we can keep ourselves pure."

She burst out laughing. "Considering my current state," she said gesturing at their babies, "purity is not our strong suit."

His grin was mischievous. "That's because you can't keep your hands off me. Look at what your naughty ways caused."

Reese buried his face in her neck and breathed in her scent.

She laughed some more at his teasing because Lord knew he was the one who couldn't keep his hands off of her. He was always touching in some way and constantly staring. "Alright, my love," she said, "let's go and find me a dress so we can get married."

They bought a simple white dress with a lace bodice with spaghetti straps and a waterfall skirt an hour later. Sarah's hair was in a half pony, and a simple brocade headband was used as a veil. They had their wedding bands engraved with each other's names at a jewelry store near the hotel.

Reese had packed his black suit, crisp white shirt, and black tie while she was in the bathroom gathering supplies for her toiletry bag, so he was all set.

They found the Clark County Marriage License Bureau and chose the package that included five digital pictures, an online photo gallery, a silk bouquet, and matching boutonnieres.

The chapel had wallpaper with gilded gold medallions covering it. There was a plant stand that was a bust of a child holding up silk plants. A band of sheer curtains decorated the front wall with a floral garland, and fairy lights lay atop.

They stood by the minister, holding each other's hands, and gazed into each other's eyes. After reciting their vows, they were pronounced man and wife by the state of New Jersey. Reese cupped Sarah's face and kissed her. When they pulled apart, Sarah had tears running down her cheeks. Reese swiped them away with his thumb.

They snapped a few photos with a professional photographer. Reese's favorite was of him standing behind Sarah with his hands resting on her belly while she held her silk bouquet.

"Come on, wifey. Let's celebrate."

They had burgers and fries at Sutton's Grill on the ground floor of the hotel. She dipped her fries in her milkshake, and he tried not to gag, which made her laugh. Reese refused when she offered him one. "Pregnant women and their weird appetites," he proclaimed as he held his hand up to decline her offer.

Their kisses were fevered on their way to the suite. He slid the key card through the lock and opened the door with one arm wrapped around her. Reese hooked the do not disturb sign on their door handle, closed it, then cupped his wife's face and thoroughly kissed her.

He hooked his thumbs under the straps of her dress and moved them off her shoulder. His hands moved to the back of her dress to find its zipper and gently tugged the puller, sliding it down. He helped her out of her dress, and she stood there in her white bra and panties.

Sarah helped him out of his clothes, adding them to her discarded pile. She ran her hands down his chest to his underwear-clad erection, where she gripped.

Reese threw his head back and groaned at the tingles that her touch left in its wake. His underwear felt a little damp. Reaching behind his wife, Reese undid her bra, then slid it off. He turned Sarah to face the wall and moved his hands to her waist to slide down her panties. He went down to his knees to help her out of them and tossed it in their pile of clothes.

"Hold on, baby," was all he said before burying his face between her legs. Sarah stuck her butt out even further to accommodate him. His tongue shot out, and licked her seam. She opened her legs wider to grant him easier access to her sex. The tip of his tongue flicked her clit and her head fell back as she moaned. He began his sensual onslaught on her sensitive clit. Her legs shook at the intensity of pleasure he created as his tongue assaulted her nub, the sound filling the room. She cried out, body jolting as she came. His tongue gave one last lick at her seam, and then he stood up.

Since her pregnancy, her body was sensitive—it didn't take too long to get her off.

She turned and positioned him against the wall. Then she knelt in front of him.

"You don't have to do this, Sarah."

"Cum in my mouth, love," she responded. He groaned as she wrapped her hands around his cock and licked up his shaft.

Then she slipped him in her mouth and took him as far back in her throat as she could manage. She withdrew and brought him deeply again. His groan was bestial, and she sucked on his sensitive shaft. Her mouth slid up and down his cock. He cried out in pleasure, and she increased the pace and her suction. His ass cheeks clenched as she used her hand to jerk him off while her mouth took him in.

"I'm gonna cum," he shouted in a strangled tone. Sarah increased the pace of her hands and felt the warm liquid shoot down her throat. She withdrew him from her mouth and swallowed his juice reflexively.

He caught his breath for a second and then hooked his hands under her arms to haul her up and held her close while their breaths steadied.

"You can use the bathroom first," Reese said, then walked over to the bed and moved the tray of choco-late-covered strawberries and swan towels off to the side.

"Thank you, sweetheart," Sarah said while the back of her hand was at her mouth.

Reese opened their luggage so that she could gather what she needed. She disappeared into the bathroom.

While the water for the shower turned on, he sat on the edge of the bed with his elbows resting on his legs and his head in his hands.

The door opened, but he didn't move. His wife hurried over to the bed to sit beside him. Placing her hand on his back, she asked, "What's the matter, sweetheart? Are you not well? Do you have a headache, or is it something else?"

"A headache, and I didn't want to say anything because I don't want to ruin our wedding day for you." He grabbed the first out she provided in an attempt to set her mind at ease.

"Alright," Sarah sighed. "Wanna call it a night?" she asked while running her hand up and down his back.

He looked at his wife and said, "How about we lay in bed, and I hold you for a while. You can eat those strawberries if you want."

They settled into bed, and he held her, but she passed out before she had the chance to eat their romantic snacks.

*T*he following Monday, we were over at Dad's apartment. His eyes bounced between the two of us as we sat on his couch.

"We wanted to tell you we got married in Atlantic City over the weekend."

His eyes widened, and his mouth dropped open. "Wow...I...wow." A shadow passed over his face and eyes.

My heart fell in response, and I bit my lip. Crap. "Aww, Dad, I'm sorry. We didn't mean to hurt your feelings. We just thought it was a good idea because we've been so busy lately. And we're going to become busier when the babies come. I wouldn't have the time to plan a wedding *and* run a business *and* be a mom."

His face relaxed. "It's that I haven't had the chance to walk you down the aisle, and I was looking forward to it."

Super crap. I tilted my head and looked at him. "Sorry, Dad." Sheesh, I never expected him to be hurt. Shocked, yes, but not hurt. It made me feel like an inconsiderate slug.

"It's okay, kiddo. I'll get over it. What's important is that you're happy with all of this." That was Dad for you. Ray Stevenson looked on the bright side, even when his heart was broken. He'd done the same when Mom was on an audition and missed our recitals.

"Yes, thrilled. We have wedding pictures available online." I opened my purse, pulled out a card with the picture info from my wallet, and handed it to him.

As he looked at the card, my eyes welled up.

He looked up, saw my tears, and moved to wrap his arms around me. "Love you, kiddo. I want you to be happy, that's all. If you're happy, then I'm happy." He kissed the top of my head and rocked me back and forth a little.

"Love you too, Dad." I wanted to take his disappointment away. Maybe there was a way to make it up to him.

～

The next day I was transferring pie trays into the oven when my cell phone went off.

Brianne Hains: You got MARRIED and didn't tell me?!?

Brianne Hains: I thought you loved me. :(

Sarah Malone: I love you, Bri. We got back two days ago, and I've been swamped at work. Plus, every time I sit down, I fall asleep.

Sarah Malone: I'm so sorry I didn't say anything yet. I'll find some way to make it up to you. **Brianne Hains:** Really? How?

Sarah Malone: Don't know. Let me think about it.

Brianne Hains: I'm coming to see you on the boat. You can make it up to me with free food.

Sarah Malone: Ok, I'll have a bunch of food ready for you. We can eat in my office away from the crowds.

Brianne Hains: Wait. You have an office? And why not with the crowds? No seating?

Sarah Malone: Yes, I have an office. And I don't like crowds because I'm afraid that someone will hit me by accident and hurt the babies.

Brianne Hains: Oh. Well, that makes sense. Hey, how are you feeling lately?

Sarah Malone: Tired and overheated. And my back hurts from hefting around your niece and nephew.

Brianne Hains: You make being preggers sound so

appealing. And... squeee!! The babies. OMG, I can't wait!

Sarah Malone: Haha...me too.

Brianne Hains: Ok Es, I have to go now. See you soon.

Well, at least I'd kind of sort of smoothed that one over. I still felt like a heel over how it went down with Dad. Would he accept food? He'd tell me it was no big deal, but I could sense that it was. Another text came in, and this time it was from Charlie.

Charlie Stevenson: Seriously, Es? Bri told me you got married. Bri. Not you.

Sarah Malone: Sorry, Charlie. :(I've been swamped since we got back. I've only told Dad, but that was it. He must have told Bri because she just texted me. Again, I'm so very sorry. Please forgive me.

Charlie Stevenson: I'll think about it. ;)

Sarah Malone: :(

Charlie Stevenson: Promise to make it up to me with free food like you promised Bri, and we're cool.

Sarah Malone: Sure. Whatever you need.

Charlie Stevenson: Love you, Es. You know that, right?

Sarah Malone: Love you too, big bro.

Charlie Stevenson: You know that, right?

Sarah Malone: Yes. I know that.

Charlie Stevenson: Good. See you around.

Sarah Malone: Ok... see you later. Bye.

By lunch, another text came in from my mom. Who told her? It couldn't have been Dad or Charlie. They weren't on speaking terms as far as I knew. That left Bri.

Gabrielle Renaud: Congrats on your marriage, Sarah.

Sarah Malone: Thanks, Mom. I appreciate it.

Gabrielle Renaud: We have to meet up sometime. I haven't seen you in a while. You must be huge by now.

Sarah Malone: Yeah, we have to meet up. Reese and I were planning some kind of reception. But with the business taking off the way it has and the babies coming due, I don't know when we'll have time for one.

Gabrielle Renaud: Let me know if you need help with the planning. I can help with that.

It could have been the hormones, but that twinge my heart. She has never done before.

Sarah Malone: Thanks, Mom. I'd like that. :)

Gabrielle Renaud: :)

I hope that my sincerity came through. If Mom wanted to try, then so should I. People needed a chance to better themselves. It didn't say much about me if I refused to give her that chance. After all, my family had made allowances for me, time and again.

The lightbulb in my head lit up.

We could have a small reception right here. We could serve food... and hopefully, I could talk Reese into catering.

Now for Carol Lynne. My stomach dropped. *Crap!* She wasn't going to let me off the hook easily. I'd have to stop by her place tonight, and I'd bring a peace offering.

Sarah Malone: Are you free tonight? I need to see you.

Carol Lynne Miller: Sorry, hun, not tonight. I'm free tomorrow night. Is that good with you?

Sarah Malone: Got a hot date?

Carol Lynne Miller: Hot, yes. Date, NO!

Sarah Malone: Really?! We really need to catch up. There's so much I need to tell you.

Carol Lynne Miller: Oh? This sounds good. What is it?

Sarah Malone: Well... I was hoping to tell you in person.

Carol Lynne Miller: Tell me now.

Carol Lynne Miller: Come on. Spill it, woman.

Sarah Malone: Well...ok. Remember that you asked.

Sarah Malone: Reese and I drove to Atlantic City last weekend and got married.

Carol Lynne Miller: Hmm...well, I guess I'm not too surprised. You're pregnant with his kids. It's only natural that you guys may want to tie the knot before the babies came.

Sarah Malone: Well, knock me over with a feather. You and my mom were the only two people who weren't upset by the news.

Sarah Malone: Thanks for understanding. :heart emoji :)

Carol Lynne Miller: What do you mean they were upset? They disapprove of Reese?

Sarah Malone: No, Nothing like that. It's more about Dad wanting to walk me down the aisle. He feels cheated out of the honor, ya know?

Carol Lynne Miller: I guess I can understand what you're talking about. Anyway, I better get ready for my date. Talk to you later.

Sarah Malone: Ok...talk to you later.

That was weird. I read over the message a few times to see if I'd said something that might have chased her off. She was usually a busybody. I might have read too much into it, because she was focusing on her date. And it was probably a date, no matter what she said.

Sarah Malone: Husband of mine, I have an idea that I want to run past you. I was thinking of arranging a small get-together with the family on the boat. Sort of like an informal reception for our family.

Sarah Malone: Spouses included, of course.

Sarah Malone: I also thought that you could handle the catering to have a proper dinner. I'll handle the pastries and coffee stuff.

Sarah Malone: Let me know what you think.

Reese didn't respond. That wasn't like him. He'd been acting closed-off lately, like this morning when I asked him if everything was okay. He'd brushed me off. Maybe he could use some time to get used to being married. I'd give him the time and space he needed to figure things out before I confronted him. And try not to stress in the meantime.

That evening, he didn't show up to pick me up, nor was Dave there, which freaked me out. After texting him and receiving no response, I walked to the subway and made my way back to our home alone.

Later that evening, he walked into the apartment while I was having leftovers by the island and reading a parenting magazine. I inhaled as I watched him, taking in that he was fine, and closed my eyes for a second. The gnawing pain that gripped my stomach dissipated.

Abandoning my meal, I ran towards him, threw myself in his arms, and held him for a time.

I jerked away and narrowed my eyes. "What happened to you? I texted you, and you didn't respond. Is everything okay?"

He rubbed his face, and his voice sounded dull. "Yeah, babe. Don't worry about it. I was okay."

"Where were you?" I was getting freaked. Maybe he regretted getting married. Lord knew he avoids unpleasantness.

"I was working late. It was back to back with no space to breathe. Sorry I didn't get back to you."

Back to back? No time? Not even to shoot me a quick text? I swallowed, and my throat tightened. "Are you... are you sure you want this?"

"Am I sure I want what?" He tilted his head and wrinkled his forehead.

"Me. This marriage. Do you think we made a mistake?" The words killed me, but we needed to discuss this.

"Of course I want this," he scoffed.

Something unpleasant snaked up my spine.

We locked eyes for a second longer, then I went to

the island, grabbed my plate, and emptied the food in the trash. After rinsing it, I placed it in the dishwasher.

"Can I get you any—"

The bathroom door closing made me glance over my shoulder to an empty room. I went over and switched on the TV, then collapsed on the couch.

After he came out, he went straight into the bedroom without saying a word. I got up and went into the bathroom to wash up and then returned to the couch, where I slept that night.

When I woke up the following morning, I was in our bed. It took a second to find my bearings because I was on the couch last I recalled. Reese wasn't in the apartment. No note, no nothing.

It felt like we'd had a huge fight. At least I knew the cause of my depression. God, how long was he going to keep this up? There was nothing else to do except go to work. Sitting around waiting for him to come home only to stonewall me wasn't top on my list of things to do.

Working was a great stress reliever, as I'd discovered recently. At least my problems didn't bother me when I was working, but they always returned when I stopped. It didn't hurt that my job was located in the one place that always brought me peace—the water.

I went into work and baked three days' worth of

minis for the bistro, then took a break in my office and fell asleep on the couch. I woke up feeling drained, like someone had attached probes to my body and emptied my life's energy. I tried to get up, but couldn't, so I laid back down and went to sleep.

When I opened my eyes, my heart stopped. A heavyset man and had slick back hair hair and a gray jacket sat behind my desk. My heart slammed in my throat as I tried to sit up, but my groin cramped. I stilled in pain. The reflection of the blade of a chef's knife caught my eyes as he expertly twirled its handle.

"Sleeping beauty is finally awake. I woulda woken you sooner, but I was busy enjoying the offerings of this place. You got any gabagool?" He gestured to the desk, a variety of food from the kitchen, and a large paper cup of coffee.

"I like this place," he gestured with his knife around the boat. He continued, "I like this food. Lemme tell you, I'm a hard person to impress when it comes to food."

I trembled and didn't say anything because whatever came out of my mouth would provoke him.

"Now, lemme tell you what I don't like. I don't like

guys screwing over my family like your husband did."
My eyes widened at this. Reese? This was about
Reese? Reese did something to these people?

Another man walked through the door with thin
black hair, wearing a gray tracksuit and a heavy gold
chain. "Hey Frankie, Boss needs to see you now."

The man behind the desk looked at him. "Hey, I'm
in the middle of something."

"Boss said now."

He heaved himself out of my chair and walked out
of the room.

CHAPTER 36
REESE

*R*eese enjoyed the brief second of wide-eyed shock in Frankie's eyes when he entered Mickie's office.

"Found out something I don't like," Mick said in a nonchalant tone. He was a fit man in gray slacks, a matching gray vest, and a white shirt.

A chill ran down Frankie's body. And he'd been in this business long enough to not like them.

"Whaddya mean, boss?"

"Turns out, the goomah is the boss. Turns out the goomah is wasting my money and ordering hits, and you work for her. Does that sound right?"

"Boss... Stugots," he gestured to Reese, "insulted my family, and my niece needed help. And family helps family. So I tailed him."

"This is your family. Did you forget that!? And you did more than tail him. You broke into the office and was about to carve the wife."

Reese blanched. *Sarah. Fuck!!!*

"Easy, easy. She's alive." Mick said to Reese.

Frankie said in a jovial tone, "Was about to perform surgery on her stomach before throwing them in the ocean."

Reese turned red. His heart was racing at warp speed and his ears pounded. He propelled himself out of his seat, tackled Frankie to the ground, and began pummeling him. Mickey pointed his gun to the ceiling and pulled the trigger. The explosion made both men freeze. Reece mentally checked himself for holes.

Mick's face was stern. "I do you a fucking favor, and this is how you repay me?!"

Reese looked at him for a moment. "My wife. My family," he said.

"They're alive! Told you already. I took care of it. I'm a man of my word."

Reese nodded and returned to his seat.

"Let the money for the repairs be added to the 15k you owe. Make it 15-5."

Reese knew he was being punished for his outburst. Plaster and sheetrock didn't cost $500. He nodded in acceptance. She was alive, and that was all that mattered. He could deal with everything else.

"Bring my money Saturday morning, seven-thirty at the docks." He gestured to the door with the gun in his hand. "Go."

Reese nodded, "Thank you," then hurried out of the room and closed the door. He walked down the hall and didn't slow down when the bang of a gun exploded a few moments later.

Reese searched Sarah's workstation on the boat to find it empty. He stopped Maggie while she pushed a cart filled with dirty dishes to the sink. "You seen Sarah?"

The brown apron-clad woman shrugged. "Last time I saw her, she told me she was taking a nap in her office a few hours ago." She continued on.

He got out his phone and hit the call button for Sarah's number while walking back to her office. The door was wide open, and her blanket was lying on the floor. He picked it up and put it back on the couch. Then he ended the call when she didn't pick up.

A glint on her desk caught his eye. Upon closer examination, a chill ran down his spine when he a butcher's knife sat on the desk among an assortment of food and a coffee cup. He breathed a sigh of relief when the blade appeared to be clean.

Reese lifted the handle of the knife with the end of his shirt. He opened a drawer, dropped it in, and closed it. Then he stormed off the boat and hauled ass to their apartment. He called his wife's name, but she wasn't there. But there was one place he knew she might be, so he opened the closet, took some of her stuff, and threw it on the bed. Next, Reese dragged their suitcase from their trip to Atlantic City from under the bed. He packed it with enough clothes for her to live on for a while. Then he went to the bathroom to pack her toiletries in a small pouch.

Reaching into his back pocket, he pulled out his wallet and took out a few twenty-dollar bills, and stuck it in the pouch in case she needed to buy something.

He grabbed an old laptop from the back of the closet and placed it in the suitcase along with a Post-it note for the lock screen combination. After he was done, he zipped the bag and set out to deliver it to his wife.

Reese's knock was urgent. Ray opened the door. His father-in-law's eyes were furious as he stepped out and closed the door, effectively blocking him from entering.

"She's not going anywhere with you."

"Sarah!" Reese called out. His voice echoed in the building's hallway.

"Take your ass home and leave my daughter out of this. You're no good for her."

Reese heard a wail coming from beyond the door, and his heart plummeted.

"My ex, Gia, called out a hit on Sarah. The under-boss found out and killed Gia's uncle. That was the guy who ordered the hit. I have to pay them 15,500k next on Thursday, or they're coming after her."

Ray's face went white.

"Do...do you have the money?" Ray asked.

"I'm good, thanks. I brought her stuff." He gestured to the suitcase. "She can't go back to the apartment for another week." His voice cracked. "Tell her I love her and..." He shook his head and was about to walk away when he remembered. "I made a will, just in case. She can sell my part of the business. There should be enough money to raise my kids in peace."

Reese turned and strode towards the elevators. The sound of sobbing coming from inside the apartment echoed in the hall of the building. Tears streamed down his face, but he kept moving.

Reese scanned the list of each aisle sign at the office supply store. After some time, he located a shelf that sold a variety of briefcases. He chose a simple attaché and paid for it.

When he got to his apartment, he ran into his room and grabbed a pair of jeans and shirts from his closet. Next, he opened a drawer on his dresser to collect underwear and socks. That's when he saw a little surveillance camera he'd bought a few years ago when he was paranoid that his roommate was sneaking into his room because his stuff was moved from the place he left it. After his fears were verified via the camera, Reese kicked the guy out.

Now the camera would serve the purpose of filming whoever was about to break into his apartment. He set up the camera on the ledge of the entrance closet. The motion detector would turn on and signal his phone if someone broke in.

After Reese checked to make sure he had everything, he locked up and left the building.

CHAPTER 37

*J*oanne's eyes went round when she opened her door, and she saw her son. She bit her top lip when her eyes traveled to the duffle bag hanging off his shoulder.

He pasted on a smile. "Can I stay here for a few days, Ma?"

"Yeah, of course," she said absentmindedly as her eyes took him in. "Where's Sarah?"

"There was a small fire in our apartment. Sarah needed to stay closer to the city because she needed to check up on the boat. So I left her with Ray, and I came here because I needed a few days rest. The stress at work was getting to me," he explained like he'd rehearsed so many times on the drive there.

Her expression turned dubious and didn't move. "Shouldn't you be taking care of your wife?"

"She's with her father. He'll look after her."

"Reese." Her tone held concern. It appeared like he'd abandoned his pregnant wife. That would dredge her unpleasant memories. But he couldn't clarify further. The less she knew, the better.

"It's only for a few days. Promise. I have to go back on Thursday for a big client that is too important." That was at least partially true. He hated the lies. It made him feel dirty.

She stepped aside to allow him in. "Did you have anything to eat?" She closed the door.

Reese took a seat at the kitchen table. "Not all day. I was busy making sure Sarah's bag was packed and making plans to take a few days off. Didn't have time."

Joanne sprung into action, taking a plate from the cupboard and setting it down on the Formica counter. She opened her small, white fridge and pulled out two plastic bowls filled with leftover pasta and meatballs in sauce. She set about emptying the bowls' contents onto the plate and heated it up in the microwave on the countertop.

He took in the outdated but cozy kitchen. A faded fruit-print hand towel hung on the oven door handle. A dish rack filled with drying dishes sat near the stainless-steel sink. The cabinets had a caramel oak finish. Being there eased the gnawing in his guy was a permanent fixture as of late.

She set down a fork and plate of spaghetti and meatballs in front of him. "Thanks, Ma," he said with a smile, then dug into his first meal of the day. Dealing with stress, he'd forgotten he was starving.

"Bernard! Reese is going to stay over for a few days." Joanne called out to her husband, who sat in the living room watching TV. "Go grab the extra fan from the basement and put it in his room."

Bernard appeared in the doorway and gave Reese a chin lift in acknowledgment. Reese returned the gesture. Bernard opened a door in the kitchen, switched on a light, and descended the basement stairs.

"I wish it was under better circumstances, but I'm happy that you're here. You haven't visited overnight in years." She took a seat opposite him and rested her head in her hands.

"Gotta keep working, Ma. You know how it is. Won't be brought down the way we were after Buzz left," he said as he twirled pasta on the prongs of his fork and speared a meatball, then shoved it into his mouth.

"Remember when Sammy needed new sneakers,

you took a job sweeping Mr. Stanly's corner store? You were always helping out, even when your dad was around. You were a good kid. Had a golden heart. That's why I don't buy that bull story about the fire. You would never leave Sarah. It's not the person you are. But I won't push because you will do right by her."

He smiled with his mouth closed, relieved. He didn't feel like talking about it anymore, so he hurried to finish his food.

Bernard was climbing the stairs, carrying a standing fan. Reese stood up and took the fan from him, and carried it up to the spare room.

After washing up, he sat in bed, picked up his phone, scrolled through his contact list. Then he called the only person he wanted to talk to.

"Hello?" Her voice sounded tentative and small, which broke his heart.

"Hi, baby. How are you?"

"Stressed. Worrying day and night about you and this... situation."

"I know, baby. Me too. The drop-off is happening on Thursday. After that, this shit should be over."

"Why can't I go back to the apartment?"

"From what I can tell, Gia is making moves against the family, and she has people in the organization helping her. They know that the only way I can get out of this is to pay protection money. Gia may get her guys to break into my apartment to intercept the money. She needs money right now if she wants to run the family."

"Isn't that dangerous? Wouldn't the boss want to come after her to protect his business?"

"Yeah. In fact, when..." Reese stopped because he didn't want to scare her.

"What? What were you gonna say?" She insisted.

"Baby, are you sure you want all this? I don't want to add to the stress."

She took a deep breath. "I'm owed an explanation about why I'm separated from my husband. All I want to do right now is sit in front of the TV with you, and I can't. Instead, I'm at Dad's, worried out of my mind about what could be going on. So please, tell me, I want...and need to know."

He obliged. "When I was there, the boss killed Gia's uncle. She may not live long, and I don't even know if she's still alive." Because the game she was playing was a dangerous one. And as shitty as it was to think it, he hoped she lost, because if she succeeded, he and his family were as good as dead.

"So, we wait until the drop-off, and this will all be over?"

He could be killed during the drop-off if Gia intercepted it, but he didn't mention that. No need to freak her out more than she already was. "Yeah, baby. Until Thursday."

"What if she comes after us after that? What do we do?" Her voice held panic.

"Then we'll probably have to move. Maybe your dad can help us get into the protection program."

She exhaled again. At least that helped to calm her. They'd both lived in New York their entire lives, so moving would be a stretch for them, but they could get used to it.

"My dad is furious right now with everything. He blames you for getting me into this mess."

"I never courted this mess, Sarah. I dated a girl in high school who turned out to be a psycho—"

"I know, sweetheart. And I'm trying to talk to him. He's scared, and rightfully so. But he'll do what he can to protect me. I won't leave here until it's safe."

He squeezed his eyes shut. "Good. I love you, baby."

"I love you too, sweetheart."

"I'm gonna go now to get some rest. I'm safe now, so don't worry."

"Okay, honey. I'll talk to you again."

They hung up. Reese was going to have to sustain

himself on hearing her voice since he couldn't hold her. That will have to be enough for now.

The next morning Reese woke up early and went to a branch of his bank close to where he lived and withdrew another five thousand dollars. The day after, he withdrew the last third of the money from another branch a little farther away from Joanne's house.

On Wednesday evening, Reese received a call from a police officer. His apartment had been broken into and ransacked. So damn predictable, he thought. Because of that, he made an impromptu decision that he hoped didn't cost him his life.

CHAPTER 38

*R*eese walked into the corner bodega carrying a briefcase and spoke to the shop owner. "Tell Mick I have his money."

The shop owner held up a finger and dialed a number on his phone. Then he lifted his head away from the phone and spoke. "He said that you ain't expected to make the drop til tomorrow."

"Tell 'em that Gia broke into my apartment tonight, and I have to meet with the police. I won't be at the site tomorrow, but I have all his money now."

The shop owner repeated his words on the phone and listened to instructions. "He said wait here, and he'll have someone come get you."

Reese breathed a sigh of relief because he hadn't

known whether they would grant him the meet. He'd cleared the first hurdle.

Two rotund men entered the bodega eight minutes later. The one wearing a black track jacket grabbed him and shoved him towards the back of the store. The guy wearing a green bomber jacket patted him down, then took his briefcase. He flipped its latches and felt under the cover and the sides and under the money. "Clean," was all he said.

They brought him to a black four-door car, opened the back door, and pushed him inside. Then the men jumped in and sped off. They led him around the side door of a building with a pizzeria in the front and walked down a narrow hallway. Bomber jacket knocked on the door.

"Come in," Mick ordered from inside. Bomber jacket opened the door, walked in with the briefcase, and placed it on the desk. Mick sat behind his desk and waited for the men to situate themselves before he began because he didn't want to speak over the noise.

He flipped the latches and did a cursory check. "Sal, count it and tell me how much is there."

Black jacket, named Sal, began counting while they all waited. "Fifteen five hundred." He returned to his place among the standing men.

"No one ever hands over money until the last

minute, so this is a surprise. Now, you explained before, but tell me again. Why so soon?"

"I had a feeling your money would be stolen, so I bugged my place and left. Got a call from the police that my apartment was broken into. Gia is after the money, so I wanted to give it to you because chances are, she would be there tomorrow to intercept it."

Mick looked at him for a moment, puzzled. "You connected?"

"No. Grew up in Bensonhurst," Reese answered.

"You seem to know something about how things go down here."

"I watch a lot of movies, sir," Reese imparted.

Mick weezed a laugh. "Fuckin' movies. Didn't do us favors, right, boys?" They laughed and agreed. Mick continued. "Alright. Everything checks out. Take 'em back to where you found him."

Both men said, "Yes, boss." They shoved him towards the door and walked out. The men walked down the long hall, out the front door, and back to the car. Green bomber jacket held open the back door for him. Reese got in, and the door was slammed shut. Both men got into the front. The car shook with their weight. Sal started the car, and they took off.

They pulled up to a stoplight when a bump from

behind jarred their bodies forward. "Buckle up!" Sal shouted over his shoulder.

Reese sprung into action, pulling the belt over his torso and clicking it into place before the second bump came harder. Both men took out their guns. He ducked as low as possible in the car, which was hard to do because the belt inhibited him.

"Hold on," Sal shouted. He reversed the car, bumping into the driver behind them. Their bodies lurched forward. Bomber jacket shouted, "Fuck!"

Sal stepped on the gas and U-turned so hard that it made the tires screech and they sped in the opposite direction. The other car did the same. Its headlights shone in Reese's eyes when he glanced out the rear window. Bomber jacket readied his pistol, turned in his seat, and pointed the gun to the back window.

Reese undid his seatbelt and crouched on the floor behind the seat before the man fired his gun. His hands instinctively flew over his head. The bullet left a hole in the window, but it didn't shatter. Peeling tires came from the distance. The car stopped. Bomber and Sal burst out of the vehicle, leaving their doors open, and ran off. Reese was stunned for a second. Why was he still there like a sitting duck?

Reese crawled over to the center console and crawled out of the front passenger door. He looked from side to side and ran down a dark alleyway that led to a sidewalk. Reese looked around for an open shop to duck into, but everything was closed. He didn't hear the clicking heels that walked up behind him.

A woman's voice called out. "Never will change, huh? Always running away?" Reese turned, his face filled with dread. Gia stood there wearing black tights, black fashion boots, and a black t-shirt.

She raised a gun, pointing it at Reese. Bomber ran up behind her with his weapon raised. Gia pulled the trigger. So did the man. Everything went black.

CHAPTER 39
SARAH

*D*ad spoke to the hospital nurse sitting behind a large desk at the entrance. She checked her computer screen and provided us with the floor that Reese was on. Connie slung an arm around my shoulder as we walked toward the elevators. Her reassurance was comforting.

The double doors opened up, and we stepped in. The ride up was slow and agonizing. I wished there was a fast-forward button on life sometimes. As soon as the doors slid open, I left my family behind and hurried down the hall. They hustled after me. "Patience, kid," mixed with "Honey, be careful." But I ignored them.

Charlie, Bri, Carol Lynne and Troy, Joanne and

Bernard were waiting there. They all stood up and came over to me. I don't even know how they knew to be there, but I was grateful.

"He's still in ICU. No word yet." Charlie said.

I took a seat by the aisle so I could see the doctor. Carol Lynne sat next to me and held my hand. She coached me through breathing exercises that calmed my frantic heart.

Everyone else scattered around the waiting room. Some watched a *House Hunters* show that played on a TV overhead. Others stared into space. Charlie was standing by a pillar. His attention never moved from Carol Lynne. My brother was not used to seeing someone into holistic healing.

A tall, balding man in scrubs and a face mask pulled down to his neck came through the double doors.

I struggled to stand up, grateful that Carol Lynne assisted. Reese's mom ran up to the doctor first.

"Mrs. Malone."

"Yes." I said as I walked up to him, joining Joanne.

"He was shot in the chest. The bullet grazed his lung, causing it to collapse. All things considered, he's lucky. They're operating on him right now," the doctor said.

"When can I see him?"

"Not sure. He needs to be out of surgery before you can see him. I have to get back. Someone will inform you if anything changes."

"Thank you," was all I could get out.

He nodded, turned, and walked away. I returned to my seat.

Lung collapse. *My god.*

The doctor said he was lucky. That was something to hold on to.

Sammy strode into the waiting area. Joanne ran up to him and cried while he held her. Connie brought me a paper cup filled with water.

"Thank you." I accepted the cup and drank, because the babies needed water.

Everyone took turns going to the cafeteria. I went with Carol Lynne, Charlie, and Bri for something to eat.

After paying for my blueberry muffin and decaf coffee, I joined my family at the round cafeteria table. The place was nearly empty due to the hour. Some hospital staff sat in the back.

I tore the wrapper from the muffin and took a bite. The muffin tasted like sandpaper, and I sipped on the coffee to clear away the taste.

"Gotta say, Es, I'm proud of how you're handling yourself. Things were horrible that first time you were here."

Bri squinted her eyes and elbowed our brother, and he squeezed his eyes shut. "Sorry. Didn't mean it that way."

He meant it.

"It's okay. Things in my life always went wrong when I freaked out, so I'm trying not to." That explanation seemed lacking, but I didn't feel like launching into a speech. They kept glancing at me while we ate.

There was a small TV mounted high in the corner of the room. We didn't pay attention until a news report came on.

Shots rang out on Mott and Hester Street earlier this evening. Police and ambulance arrived on the scene to find the body of a man lying on the sidewalk with a gunshot wound. A larger pool of blood was found further up the street. Police are still looking for the body.

We sat stunned.

When we returned to the waiting room, my mother, Gabrielle, was there. My mouth fell open. I had no idea she was in New York. She rushed up and gave me a hug, which I didn't return because I still couldn't process what was going on.

She pulled away and looked at me. "My poor baby. God, twice in a lifetime, huh? What terrible luck."

Sigh.

She wasn't there the last time I was in this *situation*. And all I could say was at least she was trying.

"Thanks for being here, Mom." My smile was tight.

I sat down, and she plopped herself down beside me. I tentatively rested my head on her shoulder. Everyone in the room stared at us.

It was nearing midnight. Dad talked Carol Lynne, Charlie, and Bri into going home and getting rest. He promised to call when the doctors updated us. They all kissed me and left.

The doctor showed up at around two in the morning.

"Mrs. Malone. He pulled through surgery an hour ago. He's in recovery and still under anesthesia, so it may take another hour for him to wake up. I can take you to see him."

Dad asked, "Will you be okay?"

My Dad had been my rock for so long. Always worrying about me. I gave him an enormous hug. "I'll be fine. You and Connie have done enough. Go home and get some rest. I'll be fine."

He smiled and rubbed the sides of my arms. "Proud of you, kid."

My smile was half-hearted, but I managed one anyway. "I owe it all to you. Thanks, and I'll call you if I hear anything."

Reese's parents and brother stayed in the room, waiting for their turn.

I followed the doctor through double doors. He stopped by the third door in the hall, turned, and gestured for me to go in.

My husband laid on the hospital bed surrounded by machines that monitored his vitals. The steady beep of the heart monitor calmed me slightly. He looked a little green, and that worried me.

"Sweetheart. It's me," I whispered as though my voice would diminish his recovery progress. "You're safe now. No one will hurt you." The words caught in my throat, and I cried silently for a while. Reaching into the side pocket of my bag, I pulled out the packet of tissues Bri had given me. It was almost empty by the time I regained control.

Looking around the room, there was a big, red armchair in the corner. With some effort, I pulled it closer to the bed and sat down.

After getting my breathing under control, I said, "I missed you so much. The last few days were torture. I waited for your call last night, but something felt wrong, and I worried. So I called your mom, and she said that you ran out of the house in a hurry because our apartment was broken into. Charlie and Carol Lynne went over to the apartment to talk to the officers.

When the hospital called me, Dad and Connie brought me here."

I didn't know why I was telling him all of this. I should have kept it light, but that was what came out of my mouth, so I kept going.

"I know things will be difficult for us for a while, with your recovery and the babies coming. Maybe we can find time to get out of the city. We could go somewhere on vacation. You've once told me you've never been west. Me neither. How about we do that? Sorta like our first family vacation."

I must have drifted off to sleep soon after because I slowly opened my eyes to find Reese's blue eyes staring at me. I got up from the chair as quickly as I could.

"Oh, my god! You're awake!" I whispered-screamed in my groggy voice.

His smile was tired.

My mouth dropped open. How long had he been awake? No one woke me. I'm going to need to talk to the nurse.

"I have to let everyone know that you're awake!"

He whispered, "Chill, baby. They visited and went home. They didn't want to wake you."

He whispered, "West sounds good for a honeymoon."

My vision swam, and my body felt light. I got up and peppered my husband's handsome face in kisses.

"*D*addy wants chips." My five-year-old daughter, Marin, held up a small bag of chips from the convenience store.

Alon, my five-year-old son, said as he held up a bag, "He loves popcorn."

I pursed my lips and sighed. "Then let's pay for it. But you have to promise to give it to Daddy when we get back to the RV."

They exchanged nervous expressions that made me giggle. Those two were the most devious people I'd ever met.

I paid the attendant in the convenience store with cash for the groceries. This lot should get us through a few more days before we needed to stock up again. Years ago, Amberly's advice about taking cash when traveling to remote places was gold. Not every store was equipped with the ability to pay with a phone, much less card-processing terminals.

I handed the bags of chips and popcorn to the kids. Thanking the attendant, I picked up the grocery bags, and we made our way to our RV. The twins took off running to the vehicle and ran inside.

Reese held the door open and took the bag from me. He placed them on the counter.

The kids ran to their bedrooms. They were probably hiding their treats before I asked them to hand them over to their dad. Which I wouldn't, but it was fun to get a reaction out of them.

While my husband unpacked, he pulled a small velvet blue box out of his pocket and handed it to me. "Happy anniversary, baby."

I gasped, took the box, and flipped open the lid. A round silver locket with an engraving of a compass on the front glimmered.

Lifting it out, I peeled open the cover. On one side, there was a picture of Reese and me when we renewed our wedding vows. We gazed into each other's eyes and were dressed in full wedding regalia. The other side had a picture of our twin babies. Their tiny, newborn faces looked pissed off.

Beautiful.

My eyes filled with tears, and I threw my arms around him. He held me, and we kissed for a while.

Our kids came out of their bedroom and said in unison, "Oooohhhh," followed by giggles.

Reese and I broke off our kiss to laugh.

I pulled away and went to my bag to pull out a package wrapped in gold, then handed it to him.

He hiked up a brow and took it from me. "You had that with you this whole time?"

I smiled and shrugged.

Reese used to tease me that my bag was so large that we didn't need a diaper bag.

He tore open the wrapping to reveal the new Forza Motorsport video game. His eyes widened, threw an arm around me, and said, "Thanks, baby."

Our kids came up to us and handed us a red card made from construction paper. It had a heart-shaped sun, water, and a boat. It said "Hopee Anvrsree."

We lifted our kids and kissed them.

Ten minutes later, we were on the road driving towards the mountains of Colorado. The sun was setting and lit the sky in golds and pinks.

***

The End

Continue on Carol Lynne and Charlie's journey.

Holistic Heat (Elements of Danger Book 2) be available for sale on March 4, 2022.

Be sure to turn the page to read about Charlie and Carol Lynne. He shows up to her apartment with Amberly's lipstick on his neck. *jaw drops*

***

Sign up for my newsletter to receive a *free* chapter as I write it, "Revved Up: Adventures of a Girl Cabbie. You've met Janine. This is her story.

To read more about it, go to:

www.willabrooks.com

***

If you enjoyed this book, I'd appreciate a review.
Thank You.

ABOUT THE AUTHOR

Willa Brooks grew up in Queens, New York sneaking her mom's historical romance novels. She also watched a ton of soap operas and fell in love with crazy storylines.

She studied creative writing in college. After taking a long hiatus from writing to raise her son with her graphic artist husband, she decided to go the indie publishing route.

She loves anything retro, and watches a ton of sitcoms from the '70s and '80s.

For more books and updates:
http://www.willabrooks.com

HOLISTIC HEAT

*T*he first thing I did when I got home from work—or as people on the commune called it, "the rat race," was take off my gold chain link necklace, bracelet, and earrings. The thump of the jewelry box closing gave a strong sense of satisfaction because they were more like dog tags than decorative. Sometimes, I like to wear my Buddha beads but not this evening because my neck was already damp with sweat. The red cotton briefs and a white cami would suffice since it was rare that people came over.

Since my best friend, Sarah, came by less frequently—well, rarely, I'd taken a shine to being half-naked. Growing up as I did on a commune, or as we called it, an intentional community, I'd be okay with being naked. But it wasn't anything like that. Besides, who in their right mind did farm work naked

Pulling out the elastic that held my blonde hair in a clean ponytail, I flipped it over, gathered it, and retied it into a messy top bun.

Not wanting to cook after my shitty day, I opened my freezer door to make a selection from the variety of frozen organic meals. My kitchen was a small fridge, a stove and a sink that occupied the space of the back wall. It looked like it was a part of the living room.

The phone binged with a notification of an incoming text. I closed the freezer and walked over to the side table by the patchwork couch to see who it was.

Charlie Stevenson: Can I come over? I'm feeling sort of down.

Carol Lynne Miller: No. Sorry, My day was fucked up. And I don't feel like having company right now.

There was a knock on my door. I rolled my eyes. Sheesh, this man took liberties whenever he wanted. There went arrogance for ya.

"Hold your horses!" I shouted at the door, then ran into my bedroom, grabbed a pair of tanned shorts from my dresser drawer, and slid it on.

I hurried out of the room while buttoning and zipping up my shorts. After turning the locks, I pulled open the door to a hulking Charlie. He stood there in brown aviator glasses, a white shirt, and tanned slacks. His hair was shorter since the last time he was here, but his beard was still scruffy.

My heart fluttered, and I promptly squashed it. Having feelings for this man was dangerous. Sure, we slept together a few times. My reactions towards him were nothing more than a memory of a great orgasm. It wasn't like I was looking for a commitment. Nor would he offer one.

"Come in and tell me about your shitty day, but you'll have to hear about mine. You're warned," I narrowed my eyes.

Charlie walked in with a faint smile on his square face. That jaw made him look like a sexy Neanderthal.

"You didn't have to rush to get dressed. I've seen you naked, remember?"

Oh, I remember. Trust me. And I tried to forget it but can't. I refuse to caress the ego of this arrogant prick. I rolled my eyes at him, deliberately being dismissive. After we had sex the first time, he was weird afterward —typing on his phone and writing notes in his book. Not gonna lie. It hurt my feelings. So, I kicked him out of my apartment.

When he talked me into it the second time, I knew what to expect and told him that he had to leave immediately after. He was too good to refuse, and as much as it pains me to admit, I needed physical contact. Needless to say, he was shocked, and frankly, I was surprised he accepted my terms. That was the second time we hooked up.

I was holding out for Mr. Right, but at this rate, I seriously doubted that he existed. Perhaps all we can hope for was Mr. Right now. *Charlie*. As he walked by, there was a red stain on his neck.

"Are you bleeding?" I called out and turned his collar down for a closer inspection.

Charlie's expression morphed from curious to sheepish. "Naw, that was from my girl."

I froze as my body burned with the fire of humiliation. I readjusted his collar, gulped and said, "I'm sorry. I should've minded my own business." I scooted away and led him to the couch as a flush crept up my neck. While we settled on the couch, I hugged my red mandala toss pillow while trying to ignore the pain in my throat. If he aired what was on his mind, he could leave, so I could finally put this shitty day to rest.

"So, what's up?" I prompted, wanting him to get this over with.

"I had a case that I couldn't find a way around

except to offer a settlement. Dad figured out a loophole in like two seconds. I'm paranoid that he'll look down on me, and I may lose my good standing as someone he'll pass the company to."

"You think he'd look down on you because he offered you a suggestion? If that's all it takes to look down on a person then—"

"Look, he's a good man, but he wants me to earn the company," Charlie cut in.

"And you think you're less deserving if he figures out something faster than you? Ray has had years of experience. I'm sure his mind is trained to pick up details that you'd miss. And so what if you're not the best lawyer, at least you're hard-working, and that counts for something, right? You can prove your worth in other ways."

He raised a heavy brow, "How?"

"Well, even if you don't win all your cases, you can still do things on the business end to make sure your dad's firm is perceived as one of the finest in the country. Find ways to drum up more business."

Charlie stared at his clasped hands, lost in thought. I just sat and watched our reflection on a TV screen. My throat chakra was blocked probably because I had been fighting a scream since I got home.

"So tell me why your day was so shitty." He interrupted my thoughts.

I blew out a breath. "I got fired today."

He reared back. Something about his reaction made me hike one side of my lips. Probably because his privileged ass figured out that there were other people with problems a little more significant than looking like a simpleton in front of your daddy. Some people didn't even know their daddy.

"What? How? You seem like the type to be diligent at work." He sounded confused.

Type. A classification. My spirits fell further. "I didn't fuck anything up. I got fired because the lady who was my competition for the job got promoted. And since we never got along—" I shrugged.

"Is there any recourse you need to take, I mean legally?"

I gaped at him. Was he offering me help? "No. They're mailing my severance pay since I have a contract."

He squinted and slightly shook his head. "Why are you so calm? Shouldn't you be in tears?"

I pursed my lips. "Saw it comin'. That was why I started this new gig in the first place. Looks like I'm going to be a concert promoter full-time. Eventually, I'd like to turn it into a charity leg of concert tours where bands can donate their earnings for that concert to charity. But first, I need to build up my reputation, so I'm working on putting together regularly scheduled shows. I have a gig tomorrow night, so I don't have time to be upset."

"Sounds cool. You told me about the concert when I drove you home from the hospital. Neat idea about the charity leg too. Hope it works out." He glanced at his Rolex and stood up. "I gotta get going."

Thank goodness. I stood up. "Thanks for dropping by." Not really, but Momma raised me to have manners even when I didn't feel like it.

"Thanks for talking to me, and I'm sorry about your job, Sugar."

Ugh. Sugar. He started calling me that after he found out I was from Mississippi. I told him to stop, but as I'd discovered, if you tell him to do anything, it only makes him do it more. I swear he grew a beard because Ray told him to shave, so he did it out of spite.

I led him to my front door and opened it. We said our goodbyes, and I closed it. Finally! I could let loose and cry without looking weak in front of people. I slipped off my shorts and returned them to the drawer when my phone rang. Oh, fuck my life!

I hurried back to the living room. After taking a

gander at the long numbers on the screen I guessed who it was, a pang of regret hit my heart as I swiped the green button.

"Hey, Momma. How're ya doing?" There was a pause before she responded in her southern accent. Her voice was deep and slightly raspy.

"Carol Lynne? You on your smartphone?"

"Yes, Momma. Is everything okay? You're calling from the payphone at the convenience store down yonder, aren't ya?"

"Oh, yeah, everything is okay over here, Sweet Pea. How about you?" Dang, she can already tell. I must sound like shit.

"Well, I got fired today." No need to beat around the bush, I guess.

"Does that mean you're comin' home?" The hope that filled her voice made my heart ache. She must've been lonely. That was what happened when you're the social pariah on a commune. The founder fell in love with my biological father. Guess who won that battle? *Free love*. Nothin' was ever free.

"No, Momma, it doesn't. I had a feeling that this would've happened. So, I started another business as a concert promoter, and I'm working tomorrow night. As much as this sucked, it wasn't the worst thing that could've happened."

That reminded me to remind Keith about the gig his band is playing tomorrow night. I didn't trust that they'll remember because their drunkenness was a common state.

She laughed good-naturedly. "That's my Sweet Pea. Like a cat, always landin' on yer feet."

"Yes, Mam. I'll be fine. But how are you?"

She sighed, "You know. Busy. Plumb tuckered."

Yeah, I know. All that manual labor with nothing to show for it. My mother was a cook in the restaurant on RiverRun Farms and works for $100 per month. I'd tried to send her money over the years, so she didn't need to spend hers, but she told me that she didn't need much to get by. I told her that it wasn't about getting by, it was about leverage. She said that she didn't need it or anything else. The only time she did was when she called and begged for $700 for a new mattress.

She hesitated. "Just callin' to check up on ya. It's been a while since we talked or even saw each other."

"I know, Momma. I might have more time now that I'm running my own business. Maybe I can come to visit for a while."

"That would be wonderful, Sweet Pea. I'd love that." The excitement in her voice tweaked my heart. I'd been such a bad daughter.

"Or, I could send you some money, so you can buy a plane ticket to visit me."

"Oh darlin', you're sweeter than sugar. But I can't get away. You're gonna have to come down here."

I frowned, "Okay, I'll do that. Love you, Momma."

She hesitated for a beat then said, "Love you too. Bye, Sweet Pea."

"Bye, Momma."

That was weird. I had this strange feeling that she wanted to say something to me, but decided not to when I mentioned that I lost my job. Sucks because I would've helped her in any way I could if she asked.

I took a bag of frozen leftover vegan chili out of the freezer and popped it in the microwave. Then I turned on my laptop while waiting for my food to heat up. The footsteps of my neighbor echoed in the hall outside. His keys jingled as he turned the lock. I got up, ran to my door, and opened it quickly before he disappeared.

I called out, "Keith, wait!" The tall, skinny dark haired man jerked in surprise. His eyes stayed wide open as they traveled down my body. My eyes followed his and looked down at my bare legs.

"Fuck!" I shouted and ran back into my apartment and slammed the door.

CPSIA information can be obtained
at www.ICGtesting.com
Printed in the USA
LVHW091916130821
695254LV00004B/19

9 781777 843212